The Spirits of Shadowfire

P.I. Fagoras

authorHOUSE™

1663 LIBERTY DRIVE, SUITE 200
BLOOMINGTON, INDIANA 47403
(800) 839-8640
WWW.AUTHORHOUSE.COM

First published by AuthorHouse 08/01/05

ISBN: 1-4208-6757-1 (sc)

*Printed in the United States of America
Bloomington, Indiana*

This book is printed on acid-free paper.

Prologue...

He sat on the monkey rock watching the setting of the two suns. You could not help but be drawn into those temptingly cool and limpid pools. His eyes were a bright and sparkling ice blue, mesmerising in their reflection of the fading sunlight. Gazing into their depths you felt your whole body leaning forward, heels lifting off the ground, as if on the verge of leaping into that fabulous abyss.

But then, just as the temptation reached breaking point, he blinked and the moment would be lost. Leaving you shaking your head to clear away the unexpected and lingering emotion, and there you would see a tired old man dressed in clothes that were once fine and expensive but now faded and, in places, a little worn.

He raises his aged hand to his wrinkled face, tanned to the colour of leather by the sun, and scratches at his head covered in fine, wispy hair then returns it to the handle of his battered staff, staring from beneath bushy white eyebrows with his astonishing eyes.

You might say, nothing much to look at; just a worn out old man. But a man with a rich tapestry of life behind him and the key to the future of his clan and all life forms in this collection of galaxies.

His name was Irises...

Chapter 1
The Beginning

TJ and Jessica hurried through the bustling streets of Neo-Anapia heading towards the academy. Irises, the clan leader was to begin teaching them new lessons at school. Jessica's father, Rathooq, had told them of Irises' legendary fighting prowess and his great wisdom.

"Do you really think Irises is as old as your dad says?" asked TJ, trying to keep up with Jessica.

"Who knows" she shrugged. "All I'm thinking about right now is how late we are going to be! How come you have to take so long to eat breakfast? Oh, I forgot you have to cram in second and third helpings before you're full!"

"I am a growing boy and besides, it's not my fault your mum is such a great cook. I just can't resist her food especially those thick buttery blueberry pancakes she makes. Mmmmmmmm! You should be grateful, my mom might be a good warrior but she is the worst cook in the whole universe."

"We're about to be taught by a living legend, whose bravery and courage are our shining example and all you can think of is your stomach!" yelled Jessica, stopping in her tracks, hands on her hips.

"I know Jess, why don't we cut through the Crooked Passage it will take at least five minutes of our journey"

"I am not sure that's a good idea T, you know we are not supposed to leave the main road" Jessica replied cautiously.

"Come on stop being a scaredy cat" TJ exclaimed as he turned down the dark pathway that ran between two tall old buildings. The fire escape on the smaller building of the two had a faulty overflow pipe above it that constantly dripped water. The staccato rhythm tap, tap; tap could be heard as it created a large puddle.

"I'm not sure about this TJ..." began Jessica but it was too late, he had already made his mind up. "Here we go again, he's always doing stuff like this" Jessica mumbled to herself. "Hold on, I'm coming!"

TJ stopped, looked over his shoulder and then waited for his friend to catch him up. As the two children approached the exit of the alleyway, they saw some teenagers sitting on the wall talking and smoking. Their Geometric school tunics were dusty and unkempt. One of them, the largest, took notice of the two children, jumped off the wall and walked over towards them, chewing gum and sniffing.

"I've got a bad feeling about this TJ" Jessica said nervously, "look; they're smoking—let's turn back"

"Oh stop being silly Jess, we're almost there now, don't worry, just ignore them they'll leave us alone."

"They're not ignoring us they're coming over!"

The leader must have been about fifteen years old. He was quite tall with bright red hair and freckles all over his face, his black t-shirt was dirty and it carried a strong smell as if he had worn it for five days; you would find yourself blinking just to make sure that flies were not surrounding him.

"Look at these two little geniuses going to their posh school. What do you think you're doing down here? Don't you know the alleyways are not for your use little man? And to think you took your girlfriend down 'ere as well"

"She's not my girlfriend" TJ replied, catching sight of three of his friends appearing from over the boy's shoulder.

"TJ lets gets out of here!"

"I'm not scared, what are five teenage boys doing trying to scare us? The alleyways are for everyone to tread if they please."

"Oh look!" the leader said over his shoulder to his chuckling friends, "this one's a bit brave, I'm gonna have to teach him a quick lesson before he starts school."

"Come on TJ!!" Jessica said once again, pulling at her friend's arm.

"No! We shouldn't have to."

At that moment the leader pushed TJ to the ground. And as he got up, the boys all began to laugh. TJ looked up at the leader, his eyes emitting two flashes, small glimmerings of light that could also be seen flashing in Jessica's eyes as well. The blue beams in the eyes of the two seven year-olds vanished as quickly as they came. The older boys looked at each other.

"What was that Jess?" TJ enquired.

"I don't know but I feel very strange. Let's go now!" pleaded Jessica.

"Okay" TJ replied.

"Too late little man, we can't just let you go, especially after speaking to me like that—I would lose face, lose the respect of my peers, and once this gets out anybody would think they can walk down here."

He picked up TJ with his bony hands and threw him against the wall with a resounding thud.

"You big, overgrown hairy bully!" yelled Jessica as she reached out and touched him. Suddenly, everything seemed to slow down, the drips of water were suspended mid-air. As she grabbed the leader, his skin tone changed colour to a shade of blue, then with blinding speed Jessica punched him and he flew into the wall. Briefly a number three appeared above his head then quickly disappeared again as he lay unconscious on the floor.

"What's happening to me? I feel strong!" TJ looked at her, startled.

The other three boys decided to attack at once. With one hand, Jessica lifted one of them into the air and threw him on top of his leader. Once again a number three appeared above his head and then disappeared. Instinctively TJ jumped up and landed two punches, catching the other two thugs on the nose, sending them both crashing to the floor. Once again a number three appeared above their heads. Simultaneously the water resumed its clockwork dripping.

As the bullies lay on the ground Jessica approached TJ with tears in her eyes.

"Come on Jess we'd best go now" he said starting to sprint.

Jessica nodded and started to run but she found she could run twice as fast as him and caught up with him in an instant. She touched him on the arm and emmediately everything slowed down again.

"What's happening TJ?"

"I don't know but now I'm so confused. If we touch each other again will this weird stuff start up again?"

"I just don't know. Do you feel all strange too?"

"A bit. I feel very strong but I'm really afraid."

"My mind is racing along I can't comprehend everything, my senses seem to going wild and

5

I'm bursting with energy" replied Jessica looking confused.

TJ then looked up at a brick wall they were passing a glint in his eye.

"Hold on Jess I want to try something," he said charging at the brick wall.

To his friend's surprise he began to rapidly scale it, but as he neared the top of the wall, the strange blue glow began to fade from his eyes.

"Oh nooooooooooo!!!!!" he cried as he lost his grip.

Jessica looked up as she ran forward and managed to catch him at the bottom. They both fell over and landed in a heap on the grimy floor, their backpacks split open and books and papers fell out scattering around them. Jessica glared at TJ and pushed him roughly so she could get to her feet.

"Oh great" she barked. "Look at me now! My new outfit is covered in dirt and my lovely new shoes are scuffed. I'm so angry I could kick you with them! I've been saving these for weeks to wear especially for today. As always you insisted we just had to take a short cut down that alleyway, you just had to try something different and climb up a wall, you just had to get us into a fight look and at me now! Thanks a lot TJ for making a mess of today!"

Jessica continued grumbling loudly she began to collect her belongings together roughly shoving her books back into her bag and hastily brushing herself down.

The one thing Jessica was most particular about was her appearance and it always drove TJ crazy, but looking at her now with grime smeared over her robes he knew that she was very close to killing him.

"Jess this feeling is amazing! Come on we've just got to hurry up and get to school. I'll race you!"

She looked up to see TJ running. "TJ wait for me!" she shouted after him as she grabbed her bag to race after him, determined not to let him win. "Today is just going from bad to worse" she thought to herself.

The two of them reached their classroom and peered inside. The whole class were seated on cushions on the floor facing Irises with their backs to the door. The old man was crossed legged in the lotus position floating above the floor. He was deep in meditation with his eyes firmly shut beneath his bushy white eyebrows.

"Come on Jess stop looking like a sour puss. There are two empty cushions right at the back of the class. I bet we can sneak in as quiet as mice and no one will notice," whispered TJ as he eased the door open.

Jessica gave him her dirtiest look to let him know once again that everything was his fault.

"Wow!" TJ thought to himself, "If looks can't kill."

They crept stealthily along the back of the room, as quietly as possible, not daring to breathe. Just as they began to believe they were going to make it to the big plump cushions, Irises' gentle voice called out to them.

"Ah, our latecomers have arrived. How nice of you to honour us with your presence, I trust that your journey was without mishap."

"Everything was fine, sir" Jessica replied, desperately trying to prevent her voice from breaking with fear and apprehension.

"Good! Unfortunately you have missed morning meditation but I'm sure we'll find some way you can make it up later in the day."

The pair looked at Irises then turned to each other. How could he have known? His eyes were still firmly shut and neither had made a sound.

"I suggest," continued Irises, "that you bring those cushions to the front of the class, plant your rear ends on them and pay attention. I am about to begin my lecture on the ways of Algebraic Warriors."

Burning with embarrassment they picked up their cushions and scuttled to the front, hiding their shame as the rest of the class looked at them and giggled.

"You're dead TJ" Jessica mumbled under her breath, her face still bright red.

Irises smiled to himself. He could sense the two children had a strong chi within them.

It had been decided long ago that these two would not be singled out for special treatment but would attend classes along with the other children.

In this way they would be allowed to develop naturally, and on their own. No doubt their extra skills and powers would reveal themselves again as their education progressed. Irises would be on hand to finetune their talents and to ensure they were kept under control. TJ was known to have a quick temper and it would not do for him to vaporise the whole class in a fit of anger.

"Now," said Irises settling back into his Lotus posture once more, "I shall continue our lecture. The rules of our way of life are simple! Every living thing in life has a value; whether it's numeric or represented by chemical symbols. We all have a value, and because you pupils were born on this planet called Earth, your attack and weakness value is the number 3, because Earth is the third planet from the sun."

TJ and Jessica suddenly looked at each other wide eyed.

"That's what we saw," whispered the boy.

"Sshhhhhhhh" Jessica hushed TJ before he could carry on.

Irises then looked up from beneath his bushy eyebrows.

"All of you children have a special ability which will develop with time. There will be times it will seem that you have superhuman strength," he said looking at TJ and Jessica, "and there will be times you cannot call on that strength because of your age and your development limit you. So you must learn the skills of combining your power using the power of crystals, your inner nature, different

P.I. Fagoras

fighting platforms and special attacks. Skills that all warriors must call upon to survive."

"What, like Pythagoras Palm?" TJ enquired.

"Indeed young man" Irises replied.

The old man continued, "Eventually, once you have completed your training, you will learn how to change your value throughout a battle but remember that energy cannot be created or destroyed but is merely changed into other forms. This means that if you merge with an ally this will take their value down leaving them temporarily vulnerable."

"Excuse me master," Jessica said, "does that mean if I merge with TJ and take the number 2 of his value that would give me the total value of 5 but would leave him only with a value of 1?"

"That's correct young Jessica! Well done. It is crucial that when you are in battle reveal your number only when its time to finish off your opponent. To do this your attack number must equal their weakness number. If it is too high you will be very powerful but too slow to land the telling blow."

At that moment a cool breeze blew into the dojo, halting Irises for a split second. Moving his white hair from his eyes, he continued.

"If your number is too low it will make you very fast but too weak to strike the final blow so remember balance is the key. Ultimately, you will learn how to use all the elements around you in order to aid you."

Irises then began to test the children's knowledge of Anapion history. It seemed their history master Shadhoo had taught them well as they easily answered questions about the mighty cities of Anapious and the civilisations that lived there. They were able to name all of the wise men and their successors, all the way back to the Krako period, which very much impressed the old man. After a break for lunch the class wanted to hear of the great battles Irises had fought in and of his brave acts. He happily indulged them, weaving tales of great warriors who fought evil with their algebraic skills. He told them of Abrath's evil forces attacking their planet, forcing the clan to flee as the weary warriors fought the invading forces. Their losses had been great and those who escaped were lucky to do so.

Cᗡᛚᛚᛚᛚᛚᛚᗡ

The enraptured children listened to the stories of the evil tyrant Abrath destroying Anapious and sweeping through her neighbouring planets leaving a wake of death and destruction behind him.

"Tell us about your battle with Abrath, Irises?" piped up TJ, unable to contain himself any longer.

Jessica cringed at his rudeness as the whole class turned to look at them. How could he be so rude and just butt in when the Grandmaster was in the middle of teaching the class. He was so disrespectful; she hoped Irises would punish him.

"All you need to know of that story my little friend is that it was more a battle of wills" answered Irises. "I'm afraid it is a victory tainted with a sense of failure and one I would rather forget. Abrath was my star pupil" he continued, with a sad look in his eyes "and to see him in such a fallen state brought me no joy. Even now my heart weighs heavy."

TJ was curious to know the true fate of his own father, he was about to ask Irises when the old man swiftly raised himself from his sitting position, his robes falling and flowing around him. Stroking his long beard he called an end to the class and bade the children good day. With the question dying on his lips TJ watched his fellow pupils gather their things, chattering excitedly.

" Come on TJ" nagged Jessica "I want to get home, this outfit will need to soak for a week with all this dirt on it!" She brushed once again at the grubby stains as she glared accusingly at her friend.

"Who cares?" he replied as she grabbed his hand and pulled him to his feet. "A bit of dirt never stopped Irises being a great warrior. I can't wait to tell Uncle Rathooq of all Irises' amazing stories."

As the pair arrived back at Jessica's house they could hear their parent's voices coming from the kitchen.

"The people of Earth are making it quite clear we're no longer welcome here," Jessica's mum Sahara sighed.

"They can't help feeling like that Sahara. They're just as frightened of Abrath as we are. Let's face it, there are only a few algebraic warriors left. I just hope we will be able to swell our ranks with graduates from the Academy soon. With Irises teaching there now, I guess things have become a little more urgent. The earthlings have yet to realise they need us as their defences will be no match for Abrath's power," explained her husband.

"I doubt it will be long before our two will begin discovering their warrior skills. Knowing what's ahead of them I almost wish they'd never graduate. Such a responsibility on those little shoulders," Sahara sighed again.

"Well if being cheeky made you a warrior, that son of mine would kick Abrath's butt no problem!" laughed Zoe, trying to lighten the mood.

Unable to listen any more, TJ strode into the room looking slightly indignant. Jessica followed close behind trying hard to suppress a snigger with little success. Rathooq rose from his chair and hugged them both giving TJ a wink.

"I want to hear all about Grandmaster Irises and what he's taught you today. Let's go into my study and get out of the way so your mum can cook us a feast for dinner," he said steering the youngsters out of the kitchen as the two women rolled their eyes and began to prepare the dinner.

Rathooq made himself comfortable in his favourite chair then listened patiently as TJ and Jessica eagerly told him of their day with Irises not mentioning, of course, their late arrival. Irises had made them clear all of the dirty dishes and empty the bins from the food lounge at the Academy at lunchtime as punishment.

"So tell me Jessica," asked Rathooq, staring at his daughter with his chocolate coloured eyes "how come you managed to get your clothes so dirty sitting in a classroom all day?"

"Oh I er, well erm....." she stuttered.

"It was my fault Uncle Rathooq I wasn't looking where I was going and knocked her over in the street," piped up TJ feeling guilty and not wishing his friend to get into trouble. "Anyway Uncle tell us of your escape from Anapious," he said hoping to distract his uncle and also longing to hear about his brave father he had never seen.

"Please dad, " begged Jessica, grateful for TJ's intervention.

"Hey guys you know it all. I've told you the story a hundred times you must be bored silly with it by now," protested Rathooq.

"Please please PLEASE!" yelled the children.

"Hey keep the noise down in there," yelled Sahara from the kitchen

"OK," grinned Rathooq his handsome face splitting into a wide grin "where shall I begin?"

Chapter 2
Exodus

"Abrath had returned from twenty years in exile, bringing with him mighty forces. First was an air attack from the Noboru Spirit Ships, and then the deadly Shentung monks quickly began to attack the defences of Anapacious. Abrath's two evil deputies Diavolon the diabolical and Bruto the Woe-bringer, known for their utter ruthlessness, led their powerful legions. "With explosions rocking the planet, the Anapions fled to the escape vessels hidden in bunkers deep beneath the planetary surface. All the algebraic warriors fought a rearguard action to try and give families as much time as possible. The loaded vessels fled towards the homeplanet Earth with cargoes of frightened refugees, leaving behind only a few vessels for the gradually retreating warriors."

"Yeah we know that," interrupted TJ keen to hear about his father "get to the good bit!"

Jessica stared at him, once more unable to believe TJ's rudeness. Poor Aunt Zoe must be so ashamed of a son who was incapable of showing any manners. To make it worse, her father found it funny.

"Ok, ok" he laughed. "Your father Ignea and I were moving stealthily from street to street of the great city, sheltering in the rubble of buildings destroyed by Abrath's powerful laser canons. We were using scatter mines to lay traps in the shadows of the blackened shell of the Imperial Military University. Hopefully they would be triggered by the Shentung troops following close behind. I was busy fitting the movement sensors whilst Ignea attached and set mines. As the last few mines were laid, we set off purposely for the hidden entrance to the monorail that would whisk us away to the last escape vessel which was waiting for us.

An almighty explosion knocked us off of our feet hurling us into the rubble and leaving our senses momentarily stunned. As my fragmented thoughts gathered themselves together, I soon realised the explosion was from some of the mines. Looking around at the settling dust, I saw Ignea raising himself up and shaking debris from his hair. Grinning a sooty smile, he waved me on and I once again ran between the ruins, dodging the laser fire from our foe's guns and praying our mines would slow them down.

Pushing through the shattered doors of the once magnificent Hibus Temple I dashed down the stone steps into the dark dank cellar. The great stone that was used to cover the secret entrance to the monorail was pushed aside, leaving a gaping opening into the dark tunnel. Plunging into the tunnel, I could see ahead of me the outline of battle weary warriors hurrying as quickly as possible towards the monorail. Helping the last few injured and battle weary souls into the carriage, I suddenly realised Ignea was not with me, so I decided to retrace my steps back up the tunnel to search for my dear friend.

Explosions from above were rocking the tunnel, causing debris and dust to fall from the ceiling. As the moments dragged on and I drew nearer to the tunnel entrance my fears grew and it seemed inevitable that he had fallen to the enemy. On the point of giving up all hope, a ragged figure limped into the tunnel mouth that was now choked with smoke and rubble. With fire licking at his armoured boots, Ignea smiled, his white teeth gleaming through the mask of soot and dirt caked on his face though his eyes seemed lifeless. I grabbed his arm and helped him back down the tunnel to the waiting warriors. We were the only two footsoldiers remaining to embark."

Rathooq paused to take a long cool drink from his beaker of juice. Smacking his lips in satisfaction, he turned his attention back to the two before him, their eyes bright with excitement and awe.

"The monorail moved swiftly along the escape route, the sounds of destruction crashing above. All the warriors stood silently swaying with the movement of the carriage. Hopelessness showed on every dirtstreaked face as they replayed the battle scenes in their minds.

Irises waited at the entry ramp of the last escape pod. He quickly helped the injured on board whilst instructing me to lay mines to destroy the monorail to ensure our foe could not easily follow us. Despite his wounds, Ignea insisted on helping me and I was grateful for his company. The monorail made its final journey back to the temple laden with explosives.

With all the warriors safely on board the entry ramp was closed and sealed ready to launch the vessel. Technicians worked at the ship's controls as the craft lifted from its launch pad, and the engines droned as power surged into them. Irises moved from warrior to warrior with words of praise and instructing the medical staff on treating the many and various battle wounds. His robes flowed and swished as he moved from figure to figure, and his gnarled wrinkled hands rested on shoulders giving instant reassurance. Coming upon myself and Ignea, he gripped our shoulders and looked at us with his bright blue eyes full of understanding. Ignea flinched from Irises' touch, a sad smile playing on his lips. Before anyone could question his reaction, Ignea stared defiantly at Irises and slowly before our eyes his shape shimmered and faded as he began to transform."

TJ could feel Jessica's body stiffen next to him as her father's story began to reach its pinnacle. Rathooq continued, his eyes no longer looking at the children but staring far away into the distance.

"In Ignea's place stood Abrath in all his foul glory. His battle armour glinted in the ship's lights and his eyes burned fiercely with pure hatred. I could not forgive myself for bringing him on board but his disguise had been so perfect that I never guessed the man I helped stagger down the tunnel was not my dearest friend. It was then that the full horror of the situation struck me as I realised that I had left my lifelong friend somewhere on the planet's battle scarred surface miles below us at the mercy of our evil foes.

I was so filled with rage that I launched myself at Abrath without thought of discipline or consequence, and foolishly revealed 360 degrees as my weakness number. Seeing this, Abrath was easily able to overpower me with a flurry of dragon blows to my head. I had earlier removed my battle helmet and my exposed temple was an easy target for his punches. Then I heard 'Circular Dragon Kick!' to finish me off as he completed a roundhouse kick comprising a full circle, knowing that a complete circle has a total number of 360 degrees. The last thing I remember is collapsing at Abrath's feet and the world turning black." Rathooq finished placing his hands in his lap.

TJ and Jessica released the air from their lungs, unaware that they had been holding their breath.

"Tell us the rest uncle!" blurted TJ, despite knowing the story by heart.

"How do I know what else happened?" grinned Rathooq shrugging his shoulders. "I was busy kissing the floor."

"Mum told you what happened" accused Jessica an easy victim to her father's teasing.

"Ah well, it smells like our feast is ready so why don't you ask her to finish the story. I might get some of the details wrong and you wouldn't want that. Also my stomach feels emptier than a lunarscape crater!"

TJ suddenly realised he too, was hungry and the thought of his aunt's delicious food temporarily distracted him from the story. He wished his mother could cook as well as she could fight!

Rathooq ushered them to the table where Sahara and Zoe were laying plates of wonderful smelling food. TJ's mouth watered and his stomach rumbled loudly making everyone laugh. Trying to hide his embarrassment, he piled food onto his plate all the while avoiding the dish of spinach that he hated. Turning his eyes imploringly to his aunt, he begged

"Please finish the story of the escape from Abrath, Aunt Sahara. Uncle Rathooq insists you tell it so he can eat."

"Oh does he now?" said Sahara, turning her almond shaped eyes to her husband in a mock glare.

"Well, as I explained to the kids, I was out cold after bravely facing up to Abrath so I didn't see what happened. I wouldn't want to get any of it wrong and poor Zoe here was in the sick bay so she didn't see what happened either. That leaves just you I'm afraid. Now how about someone passing me some of that buttered corn and some slices of that that Gozan lizard before I die of starvation.

"Well here's the deal then," said Sahara turning back to the children, "I'll tell you the rest but in return you will eat some of this sea spinach which is full of vitamins that growing warriors need, and, " she added, "you will both also do the dishes. Deal?"

"Oh man! Spinach is disgusting," cried TJ scrunching up his face in disgust.

"It must be bad for him not to want to eat it" said Jessica, squirming.

Neither wanted to mention the fact that it would be the second time today they had to do dishes. It would only entail a lengthy interrogation as to why they were being punished and would no doubt followed by a very early bedtime—without hearing the end of the story!

"Okay, no deal then" replied Sahara, picking up her fork and tucking into her food.

"Oh please Aunt Sahara," begged TJ, using his cutest eye-gaze on her.

"Nope. You guys know the deal. Take it or leave it".

TJ and Jessica looked at each other then sighed. "Ok you win we'll eat that disgusting slime!"

"Good" she replied making sure she scooped an extra big spoonful onto their plates. "Tuck in guys! You know spinach tastes worse cold," she laughed watching them both gingerly taking tiny mouthfuls and grimacing. Pouring juice into everyone's beakers, she picked up the story from where her husband left off.

"I had been in the sick bay on the escape pod when Abrath made his transformation," she began. "I left Zoe having her wounds treated and returned to the hold to see if I could help. It was a complete shock to find Irises standing before his former pupil, glaring at him with his stunning blue eyes. Abrath looked a little different from when I had known him at the University, a little colder and more brutal. "

"Surely you couldn't believe I would never return?" Abrath had sneered.

"I knew you would return someday Abrath. You were always a determined pupil, hungry to achieve your goals. Yet once again my dear student, you will fail to achieve what you so desire," replied Irises, shaking his head sadly.

"You are an old fool if you thought I would let you escape me. You will die here today along with these fools that follow you like sheep, but not before you give me that which I desire. I want Shadow Fire!"

Sahara looked at her audience held spellbound by her tale.

"A gasp of horror came from the bedraggled warriors watching the drama unfold before them. I tried to push through to reach Rathooq" continued Sahara, looking at her husband lovingly, "but it was impossible. Irises sighed wearily looking at the powerful armoured figure before him.

"Once again Abrath I must refuse your request. The ancient art of Shadow Fire has only been taught to one trustworthy warrior in all of history. I will never reveal its secrets to someone with a heart as dark as yours."

"So be it old man. I hope you are a more worthy foe than this pathetic heap," sneered Abrath, kicking the prone figure of Rathooq. "At least his friend Ignea put up a decent fight but my student Diavolo soon finished him as I will now finish you."

"Ignea was a far more worthy warrior than you will ever be," said Irises, "he had something you will never have. Honour!"

TJ looked at his mother; her eyes had filled with unshed tears but her jaw was set firm. She was so proud of her husband and missed him greatly. TJ was sad to see his mother so unhappy and looked back at his aunt as she continued the tale.

"Then Abrath yelled out the algebraic battle cry: "Prepare to feel the blade of Atropos!""

All of the warriors rose to their feet, ready to take up Abrath's challenge but Abrath was too fast for them and quickly created an impenetrable force-field shield around himself and Irises leaving the warriors unable to render assistance. Irises became concerned with the safety of the passengers on the vessel and instantly teleported himself and Abrath to the chosen battle realm arena, a transparent cube floating in space. The cube was transparent so light passed through it without distortion allowing us on the nearby vessel to see perfectly what was going to happen next as we crowded to the craft's windows. Due to small amounts of oxygen in the cube, only the hardiest of masters could survive any length of time in its difficult environment and Abrath's senses were sluggish to adjust. Knowing Abrath's stamina would far outlast his own, Irises decided to strike first and took advantage of Abrath's momentary confusion by unleashing a flurry of quantum punches and kicks upon his floundering protégé. Hoping to weaken his opponent, his arms and legs flew through the air with easy, fluid movements so skilfully that the watching warriors believed victory would be easily won.

Abrath reeled from the blows, desperately gathering himself together, as he quickly realised Shadow Fire was not his only lack as he struggled to fend off the blows. Rising up he unleashed a fearsome smash of tectonic-collision proportions at the old man's body. Irises, seeing the attack, dived to the side but not quickly enough to evade the force of the smash that glanced off his shoulder leaving his whole arm useless and wracked with mind numbing pain. Abrath's eyes were now wild with madness and all watching knew Irises was fighting for his life.

Locked in a titanic battle with his adversary, Irises felt a surge of rejuvenating energy and recovered his senses quick enough to see a tendril of Eldritch energy snaking towards him from Abrath's battle glove. Staring in true horror, Irises raised his hands releasing an anti-matter blast strong enough to destroy the deadly energy.

"What madness is this?" he yelled at his pupil. "Truly you have strayed from the path of good and just. Never have I known such a dark art as Eldrich used by a true warrior. Be gone with you foul being. The stench of your evilness fills my nostrils and sickens my soul!"

He raised his arms in a swirling motion and created a crushing force around Abrath's armour clad torso forcing Abrath to reveal his weakness number of 180 degrees. Unable to move, Abrath glared at his former tutor.

"You cannot destroy me. I am too powerful for you old man!" he howled, writhing against his restraints.

"Indeed you are" replied Irises his blue eyes burning with anger, "but I can make things very very unpleasant for you."

Suddenly the old man yelled "Pythagoras palm!" as his gnarled hands swirled in the air.

Before our eyes Irises multiplied into three and all three figures struck Abrath at the same time, creating an isosceles triangle of power to his solar plexus. All the angles of this straight-sided triangle; in this case being 90 + 45 + 45; totalled 180 degrees; which equalled Abrath's weakness number and sent him crashing to the ground. On the verge on unconsciousness, Abrath watched in horror as his former master wrapped him in huge and powerful kinetic chains then created a portal through to an ignominious void of sub-space into which he sent his former pupil.

Powerless to stop himself, Abrath felt his body being sucked into the void—his terror and humiliation showing all too clearly for all to see on his scarred face. Without a backward glance, Irises unsealed the transparent cube and easily dismantled the force field to return to his battle weary warriors."

Silence greeted Sahara's concluding words even though TJ was convinced that everyone could hear his heart thumping against his ribs.

The story had ended but the questions had not.

"So how has Abrath managed to escape from there?" asked Jessica looking puzzled. "Why didn't Irises just kill him while he could?"

"No one knows why Irises let him live. It's a total mystery and no one dares to ask him. Maybe it's simply because its not our way" replied Zoe, "and with someone as powerful as Abrath, the kinetic chains wouldn't have been able to hold him forever. But it gave us time to escape to Earth and prepare for the onslaught of Abrath's revenge."

"So....." began TJ.

"No that's enough for one night" interrupted Sahara, cutting him off. "You two need to eat up that lovely cold spinach and then there are all these dinner dishes that need to be cleared up."

The adults ignored the protests from the children and retired to watch the sunsets, lost in their memories and thoughts of their close escape from Abrath.....or was it?

Chapter 3
QUANTUM ENTANGLEMENT

The class filed noisily into the large, padded dojo. This was where the older students practised their highly sophisticated acrobatic manoeuvres, leaping into the air for high kick attacks and twisting somersaults ending in flurries of punches. The padding protected them while they perfected their movements. TJ liked to watch the older students practising. His eyes would dart around, following the swift movements as the students were put through their paces by Kava, a strict and demanding teacher. TJ could not believe they were finally being allowed to use the padded dojo; he was so excited.

Kava walked into the padded room and immediately the class fell silent fearful of the intimidating reputation of the master. Unfortunately TJ and his stocky friend Chak were too engrossed in bouncing each other off the sprung walls to notice the arrival of Kava. Their giggles and squeals drew the attention of the master who glared at the pair with his steel grey eyes.

"When you two are quite finished!" he said with icy coldness frosting the edges his voice.

TJ and Chak spun round to face the master, cringing under his intense gaze.

"Sorry sir" they stuttered.

"How dare you show such disrespect for the dojo? This is a place of learning not a travelling galactic circus!"

Both boys decided it was a good time to take great interest in their shoes and bowed their heads whilst the rest of the class tried to stifle their giggles. Jessica looked at TJ in despair. Somehow he always managed to get into trouble of some kind.

"I believe extra assistance with the clearing up of the food lounge is always welcome" said Kava witheringly, "ensure you both report there after you have eaten lunch. Maybe it will inspire you to behave next time."

"Oh man!" TJ thought. Cleaning dishes two days in a row. It was so unfair! Anyway where was Irises? He was supposed to be taking the class, not meanie Kava.

"Irises will be here shortly. Please move to the edge of the dojo—and no talking," instructed Kava.

IJ shuddered. How had kava known what he was thinking? It felt so weird. Surely it was just coincidence. Please it had to be a coincidence.

The class moved to the edges of the room and waited patiently. They looked at each other with puzzled expressions but did not speak for fear of attracting further wrath from Kava.

The atmosphere in the room began to change; the air seemed to become charged with electricity. The children could almost feel it crackling in their hair. A gentle breeze brushed against their faces and a flash of colour swirled and danced slowly taking shape until Irises stood before them.

Jessica stared in awe. How had he appeared from thin air? It was fantastic. The class let out a gasp of surprise, which turned into giggles as the old man gave them a wink of a wrinkly eyelid beneath its bushy white eyebrow.

TJ could feel a pinching pain in his arm and looked down to find it being gripped tightly by Chak. How on Earth his friend would ever be a warrior mystified TJ for Chak was the biggest coward in the school. Maybe Chak had some hidden talents but they certainly had to be well hidden as no one had yet seen them.

"Let go Chak! You're cutting off the blood supply to my hand" TJ hissed through gritted teeth, desperate not to attract Kava's attention.

"Oh sorry" gasped his stocky friend, releasing his sausage fingers from TJ's arm, "that really spooked me. You would think we'd have some kind of warning. I could have had a heart attack or something. You know how bad my health is."

TJ rolled his eyes as Chak proceeded to cough feebly. As well as being the number one coward, he was also the number one hypochondriac—much to the annoyance of his classmates.

"Settle down now" called Irises above the chattering of the astonished class. "What you have just witnessed is the Algebraic Skill Quantum Entanglement also known as Teleportation."

The children all stared at Irises, totally dumbstruck. Teleportation had always been a myth and their parents rarely said much about it. Yet here, without warning in front of their astonished eyes, it had just been demonstrated by Irises.

"I know that it is probably a little amazing for you to realise that teleportation actually exists" explained Irises straightening his robes and disentangling his beard, "but there are reasons why it is kept secret, as you will find out. Master Kava is kindly letting us use his superbly equipped dojo for your first few lessons in Teleportation as your initial attempts will probably be a little clumsy and the padding should prevent any injuries" he chuckled.

TJ noticed Chak slowly turning a worrying shade of green. He hoped he was not about to throw up, as Kava would have a serious failure in the sense of humour department!

"It'll be ok Chak. Don't worry. Irises won't let anything awful happen to us; come on Algebraic warriors' teeth don't chatter, man!"

"You know," stuttered Chak; "maybe I'm getting a cold or virus or something. That's why my teeth are chattering. Maybe I'd best go home and rest."

"Watch it. Kava's looking this way" whispered TJ. "Don't want to be doing dishes all week now do we?"

TJ looked across and Jessica and grinned. She looked excited too. This was going to be a brilliant lesson.

"Teleportation" continued Irises "is a closely guarded secret. Normally you wouldn't learn this technique until your final year before graduating. Unfortunately Abrath's increased activities on the outer fringes of this planetary system have forced us to increase the speed of your education."

The children continued to stare in stunned silence.

"Teleportation is an important part of any warrior's repertoire but as well as its strength it has a weakness too. A warrior has to focus his mind to communicate to each of his body's atoms that they need to disassemble. In order to do this they must freeze in time. As the frozen suspended cells are mentally transported the warrior is vulnerable and has no means of self-defence. In addition, the time frozen cells create a ripple in time itself, similar to ripples on a pond. Anyone or anything that possesses Algebraic powers can easily detect these ripples. Not only are they able to detect teleportation and its position, they are easily able to calculate the weakness number of the transportee."

Irises paused, looking at each child in turn. He was amused to see a slightly terrified look in their faces and, hiding a smile, he continued.

"Maybe that will explain to you why Teleportation is not discussed outside of these walls. Each warrior knows how to use this manoeuvre but never uses it for fear of unwanted detection. No need for you to look so worried. Throughout the structure of this building are scattered rare and precious Lumbia crystals, which can soak up those ripples so we can practice Teleportation here without fear."

An audible sigh of relief could be heard from the class. Jessica raised her hand in the air to attract the attention of Irises.

"Yes young Jessica?" he said, catching her eye.

"Why don't warriors just carry Lumbia crystals in their battle amour? Then they could teleport without fear of detection."

"A good question my young warrior. Lumbia crystals are the heaviest crystals known and the amount needed to protect a warrior would mean them carrying over five times their body weight in crystals. So I'm afraid it is just not practical."

"Oh, I see," replied Jessica, a little disappointed.

"Now to begin with, I will teleport myself and two children from this room and then back again, then two more and so on and so on until you have all had a turn and will each know how it feels. Then we'll begin the hard work of teaching you to teleport yourselves. Who's first?"

Never wanting to miss an opportunity for a novel experience, TJ stepped forward to volunteer.

Looking around he realised that no one else had moved and tried to catch Jessica's attention but for some reason she was looking everywhere else but at him.

"Well volunteered" beamed Irises. "Why don't you bring your friend next to you here too?"

"Sure" grinned TJ grabbing Chak's sweaty hand.

Chak tried to pull away from TJ. He had no desire at all to be teleported. Supposing all of his frozen body cells forgot how they had to fit back together. Imagine, he might find his hands were on the ends of his legs and his feet were where his hands should be! Or if his body reassembled itself the wrong way round to his head and legs. He did not even want to think of the horrible possibilities should his private parts or his rear decide to be somewhere else!

"Don't worry young man" assured Irises "your body cells will fit back together like a glove. Come over here" he said reaching out a hand.

"It's weird," thought Chak "it was almost as though Irises knew what I had been thinking. Oh please tell me I had just thought it and not been talking out loud!"

Before he could think anymore, he found himself standing next to Irises and holding his hand. TJ was holding his other hand and grinning like mad.

"This is gonna be soooo cool" he whispered.

"Hush now" said Irises. "I want you to imagine each of your tiny body cells slowing down. Take nice deep breaths and relax, closing your eyes."

Both did as they were told and instantly they began to feel a strange tingling sensation all over their bodies. Almost as soon as it began the feeling left.

"Take a deep breath and open your eyes," said Irises.

TJ opened his eyes and was amazed to find himself no longer in the dojo but in the empty history classroom.

"Wow" he gasped turning to Chak whose eyes were still firmly closed. "Hey open your eyes and look where you are!"

"I can't".

"Yes you can. Just do it".

"Ok, but you have to do something for me first" Chak whined.

"What?" said TJ sighing with frustration.

"Are all my parts in the right place?"

TJ looked at his friend as though he was mad.

"Well you're still ugly and look like you could do with eating salad for a week so I guess it is all in the right place," replied TJ with a grin.

"Hey no need to be so rude" replied Chak gently opening his eyes just enough to look around. "Wow," he gasped, "that is so cool and it didn't even hurt."

"Of course it didn't hurt," said Irises. "Take my hands, we need to return so the others can have their turn."

The boys took hold of Irises hands and were once again teleported back to the dojo where their classmates greeted them.

Jessica was relieved to see TJ return safely even though she had never really doubted the skill of Irises to do what he said. She laughed as Chak began to act the hero even though they all knew he had been terrified. The two boys returned to their places at the edge of the dojo.

All of the students took turns to be teleported with Irises. Jessica took her turn with her friend Ivey. The tingling sensation made the girls giggle and Irises could not resist smiling at the two chuckling girls.

By the time the last students had been teleported, Irises face looked tired and drained. Kava dismissed the class for lunch and helped his old master to his study to rest.

"That was too much for you, Irises" berated Kava. "It is exhausting enough for a warrior to teleport himself let alone a class full of children.

"I know. It has truly sapped all of my strength, I am not a young man anymore and I'm rather out of practice" Irises replied, smiling feebly. "Sadly these children will not have the luxury of time on their side for learning. Abrath is closing in and we need to work fast. If that means tiring myself, then it is a small sacrifice."

"You can't afford to be at your lowest ebb. Who knows what Abrath will do? You will need your strength to defeat him."

"Very true my friend. Now I need a little peace and quiet and maybe a small nap to recover my strength. This afternoon we'll work on getting them ready to teleport themselves. In the meantime you might want to get yourself something to eat and check up on those boisterous lads you have volunteered for lunch duty" he chuckled, waggling his eyebrows.

TJ and Chak were the last two to file back into the dojo after lunch. Jessica tut-tutted, noticing TJ had managed to spill food down himself—she was sure she could even see the end of a noodle poking through his hair!

"I'm really, really sorry" said Chak, apologising for the thousandth time.

"Chak shut up. Sorry is not going to magically remove the food from my shirt. I hope I never have to do cleaning duties with you in the food lounge ever again".

"But I really am so sorry. The floor must have been wet I couldn't stop myself slipping. I felt really stupid laying flat on my back on the floor."

"Not as stupid as I did when that loaded tray you were carrying slammed into me. My mum's going to go mad when she's sees this mess" he moaned, looking down at the debris firmly stuck on the shirt.

Jessica, who seemed to be having a problem with her eyes, caught TJ's attention. She kept looking at him then rolling her eyes in her head. He was trying to work it out when she did it again. Frowning, he looked at her and then shrugged his shoulders. She flicked her eyes upwards once more so that only the whites were visible. He wanted to go over and ask her what was wrong but Kava would be arriving at any moment.

"What is she doing?" he puzzled, reaching up to scratch his head in confusion. His hand touched upon something cold, slimy and long. His imagination instantly went into overdrive and the only thing he could think of that would feel cold, slimy and long was a marsh leech. Immediately he imagined one sitting on top of his head ready to lunch with its suckers and, with a yell, flicked the horrid thing out of his hair.

He watched as in what seemed like slow motion, the harmless, greasy noodle flew across the room towards the doorway through which was stepping at that precise moment the grim figure of Kava. The whole class looked in horror with their mouths open as it flew on a direct collision course and neatly slapped Kava's cheek. It stuck firm for a few seconds—which seemed an absolute lifetime—then slowly slid down his face leaving a slimy trail of grease behind it.

Jessica covered her eyes in despair as Kava's face managed to change through several spectacular shades of red to raging purple. She had tried to warn TJ but once again, he had managed to get himself into trouble.

"You, boy!" roared Kava, pointing his long finger at TJ. "You will be on cleaning duties for a month and not just in the lunch lounge but after lessons too, where you can help with the cleaning and storing of training equipment."

TJ looked horrified. He was going to be in so much trouble at home and it had been an accident. He glared at Chak whose mortified feelings were reflected by the look of shock on his face.

Wiping the slimy smear from his cheek, Kava instructed the class to line up along one side of the dojo. Irises came into the room looking refreshed from his rest and seemingly unaware of the incident that had taken place.

The children did as Kava instructed them and lined up in an orderly fashion against one of the walls. Irises stepped forward and smiled at the class.

"I want you to close your eyes and concentrate on my voice alone. Remember teleportation is a difficult skill to master and this is only your first attempt so no one is expecting miracles."

The children could hear Irises robes rustling as he passed them by. His voice travelled to the end of the dojo.

"Now relax your bodies and empty your minds. Focus on each group of cells in your body from the top of your head to the tips of your fingers and toes.

The class obeyed his instructions and gradually their breathing became deeper and more relaxed. They were slowly falling into a form of meditation.

"Those cell groups you can see in your minds now need to separate so begin separating them piece by piece, using your mind's eye" Irises said, with his gentle and soothing voice.

Jessica could feel her breathing deepening and her chest rising and falling. Everything felt so peaceful. She could imagine the cells of her body joined together like a jigsaw and slowly she began to separate the pieces leaving them floating around aimlessly.

TJ too, was feeling so relaxed he was sure his legs would turn into jelly and he would fall over. In his mind's eye he imagined his cells stuck together with sticky glue and having to be prized apart. As the pieces slowly separated, he could feel his body buzz and tingle as Irises' voice penetrated his slightly foggy senses.

"You should now feel as though electricity is flowing through your bodies in exactly the same way as you did when I teleported you. Again using your mind's eye, I want you to imagine moving those separated cells through the air to the other side of the dojo. No need to open your eyes" said Irises as some of the students eyelids began to flutter, "your mind's eye will show you all you need to see."

Kava and Irises watched as the room began to fill with electrical atmosphere and the children's shapes began to become distorted and blurry around the edges.

"Once you have moved your cells to the other side of the dojo, let them join together of their own free will. Don't force them; they know what to do" he continued as one by one the children faded and disappeared.

Irises smiled at Kava whose usually fierce expression slipped to reveal a smile of relief. Teleportation was a very difficult skill to master and the class had got off to a slow but good start. Hopefully they would begin appearing again soon on the other side of the dojo.

Once again an electric atmosphere made the backs of Irises and Kava's neck prickle. Slowly, one by one, a sparkle of colour and a hint of a shape began to appear. First to fully take shape was TJ taking Kava by surprise. The boy could not help but grin as he looked at his two tutors.

Gradually the others took shape. One or two had obviously rejoined their cells too high and they reappeared halfway up the dojo wall floating in the air. Luckily the padded floor softened their fall and they tumbled down in a heap.

Jessica reappeared just along from TJ. Teleportation had created a weird effect on her long flowing hair, which now stood out on end filled with static electricity. TJ laughed as he watched her trying to tame her wild mane with little success. She glared at him as she gave up fighting her locks, sighing in frustration.

Everyone had teleported with varying degrees of success. The only one left to reappear was Chak. The class began to fidget and murmur, anxious about their classmate.

"Settle down and be patient," said Irises "it takes some longer than others to begin with. With practice you will all eventually be able to teleport in the blink of an eye. Now, quiet please; I believe our young friend is about to rejoin us."

Once more an electric atmosphere flowed through the room although this time it was much weaker. TJ looked at Jessica, his eyes revealing his concern for his tubby friend, but she was too busy coping with her hair that was going mad in the new wave of static to notice.

Slowly, next to TJ a cloud of colour and shape began to appear. Although rather worrying, the cloud was generally a pinkish colour. Across the room a separate small cloud consisting of blue and green was taking shape. The class looked at Irises in concern but his face remained unmoved though his eyes glittered beneath their bushy eyebrows. TJ became convinced that Irises was trying not to laugh.

Finally, Chak's cells appeared next to TJ. His cells had rejoined perfectly but minus any clothing. Feeling a cool breeze on his naked skin, Chak quickly covered himself with his hands while his face turned an amazing shade of scarlet.

TJ could not help but join in the laughter of the class as Chak looked about for his clothes and spotted them in a heap at the spot where he had begun his teleportation. Hobbling over awkwardly he scooped them up and quickly dressed in the corner.

"You've learnt a very important lesson today young man," said Irises addressing the wobbling figure of Chak struggling to put on his tunic. "You have to move the cells of your clothes too! Today it didn't matter but in the future it may be vital to reappear with your body amour on and weapons by your side."

The children grinned and cheered as Chak rejoined them, a little flustered but now fully clothed.

"Since that wasn't such a bad attempt, why don't we have another try?" suggested Kava his steel grey eyes wandering over the class.

Once again the class lined up and fell into deep meditation and one by one they disappeared. First to reappear was Jessica. She had completely given up on her hair and now looked as though she had been caught in a whirlwind.

"Next time I'll get mum to braid my hair so it has no escape" she thought, as she tried to tuck some of it behind her ear.

A thud sounded next to her as her friend Jasmine once again tumbled down in a heap. Picking herself up and straightening her clothes, she grinned at Jessica.

"Oops, I forgot to rejoin my cells on the ground" she laughed "am I glad this floor is padded!"

"Oh dear" replied Jessica "looks like you managed to get your shoes on the wrong feet too."

Jasmine looked down at her feet, which were pointing outwards like ducks' feet. Laughing, she dropped down and removed her shoes and put them on the correct feet.

"That's better," she said, smiling at Jessica as around them their classmates reappeared.

Some of them, like Jasmine, had forgotten not to rejoin their cells in mid-air and tumbled to the floor. Aya went one better and somehow rejoined her cells upside down. Luckily Kava stepped forward and caught here before she landed on her head.

Chak managed to reappear this time fully clothed—much to everyone's joy and relief. After all there is only so much flesh a person can take in a day.

Kava instructed the children to sit down and listen carefully as Irises had some very important things for them to remember before they could finish for the day.

"Teleportation is an important tool for a warrior to have, but it does have its limitations and disadvantages. Most warriors are unable to teleport far, very few are so skilled that they can cover huge distances. As I have explained before, teleportation creates ripples in time which can be detected by Abrath and his evil minions."

The class looked at Irises, their faces mirroring his serious face and concern. Irises was glad to note their attention for it was important that they remembered all of these details.

"A warrior is not capable of combat whilst teleportingting and is vulnerable to attack" he continued, as he watched the children begin rubbing their heavy lidded eyes.

"It is also physically and mentally exhausting. I'm sure you'll agree." He smiled.

TJ nodded in agreement as he let out a huge yawn that made his eyes water.

"You will never be at full combat strength after teleporting and it can take hours to recover. You must only use teleportation as a last resort when escaping. Always remember that," he said, sighing. "Now teleportation is only to be used within the school, it is not to be mentioned outside and I have no need to tell you of the consequences should you choose to disobey me."

Kava nodded, looking very serious as if to endorse Irises' warning.

"I'm very proud of you," Irises said, lightening the mood. "You have done very well today and I'm sure with more practice you will all be perfect."

With that, he dismissed the exhausted children who shuffled outside to collect their bags.

"Don't forget to tell your mother that you'll be late home for the rest of the month TJ. I haven't forgotten your kit cleaning duties" called Kava.

"No sir" replied TJ gloomily.

His mother was going to go mad. She would never believe it was an accident.

CRITICAL

The last month had been misery for TJ. He was so glad his cleaning duty punishment was almost at an end. As he had predicted, his mother had had a fit when he told her he had to stay after class in detention for Master Kava. She never even gave him a chance to explain.

He foolishly believed he had gotten off lightly when she grounded him for a month but she had contacted Irises and asked if TJ could bring home extra homework so he could use his time at home more constructively. Oh, she was mad with him allright.

Sighing, he closed his history book and added it to the stack of volumes on the corner of his desk. Who really cared about the ancient trade routes of Anapacious? It was all gone now, destroyed by Abrath. The things a warrior really needed to learn about were bravery, skill and as many deadly attacks as possible.

He still had his galactic navigation homework to do but decided instead to find the Kaptin Krang comic that Chak had given him. It was obvious that Chak was feeling guilty for helping to get TJ into trouble. Only yesterday he had given TJ a pouch full of starbomb sweets, knowing that they would be greatly appreciated, as Zoe never have allowed her son to have them.

He found his comic rolled up in the bottom of his bag and rummaged a bit more until he found his last starbomb. Popping it into his mouth he lay back on his sleeping pod and began reading about the all action adventures of Kaptin Krang. He was just enjoying the fizzy, sour sensation of the sweet as its hard outer shell dissolved when his mother called out to him.

"I hope you're doing that homework TJ," she yelled. "I don't want to have to come in there and check up on you!"

Trying hard to swallow the foaming remains of the sweet he yelled back "I'm doing it mum; don't worry."

He began to cough and splutter and his eyes streamed with tears as the bubble of fizz seemed to go up his nose.

"What's wrong TJ? You sound like you swallowed a starbomb and it's gone down the wrong hole."

TJ's eyes opened wide in fear. Sometimes he could swear that woman could see through walls. If she caught him skiving he would be dead. If she caught him skiving and eating a starbomb well he'd be double dead.

"I'm fine" he choked. "Just think I've caught a bit of a cold. Probably because Kava made me clean out the ice rooms today."

He coughed some more just to make it sound a bit more convincing. TJ smirked to himself. He could really think on his feet sometimes. She had no idea what Kava had given him to do so he was safe. Mind you, he had felt having to clean the entire sweat covered floor of the shadow dojo with the smallest sponge in the world had been excessive punishment. The smell still clung to his nostrils.

"That's strange" she said, a puzzled tone to her voice. "When I saw Irises today he said you'd be cleaning the floors of one of the dojos to keep you out of trouble."

"This is not good" thought TJ, grimacing. To be caught skiving, eating a starbomb and lying would be the end of the world. She really would kill him.

"Well I was supposed to but some of the older students were still practising and Kava didn't want to disturb them so he gave me the ice rooms to clean."

Stuffing his comic under his pillow he returned to the desk and opened his galactic navigation chart. His navigation master, Leps, had instructed him to draw a copy of the Noburou system, labelling all of the stars, planets and the areas of gravity traps. Gravity traps occurred where several of the planets and their large number of moons were positioned close together. The close proximity of several different gravity fields created pockets where a vessel could be trapped unable to escape, or would simply be torn apart.

Unless Abrath had a heart attack or choked on his food there was no chance of TJ ever returning to the Noburou system and it seemed pointless just copying star charts.

The door to his room slid open and Zoe came in carrying a beaker of monterberry juice and a plate of oatmeal cookies.

"Since you're feeling a little under the weather I thought something to eat and drink would make you feel better".

Smiling, she placed the tray next to TJ and watched him grab the beaker of juice and gulp it down. Looking over his shoulder she saw his study book and star chart open.

"Oh, see you've left your favourite subject to last" she said, raising her eyebrows.

"It's not that I hate it, I just wish we would cover systems nearer to Earth. I don't see any point in covering all this system when it's light years away and we'll probably never see it."

"You know TJ, you never know when some things are going to come in useful and you should pay attention to everything that's taught to you. A warrior has to rely on his wisdom and knowledge to survive. So, you're studying our planet's system I see" she said, picking up the star chart and studying it carefully before putting it back before her son.

"Your planet, mum" he grinned, "I've only known Earth as home."

"Oh Anapious is really your planet too, sweetheart. After all that's where you were created."

TJ felt his cheeks burning. He always got embarrassed when people talked about love and babies. Zoe had wandered over to his sleeping pod and was gently straightening the crumpled covers. His eyes widened in horror as her hands moved towards the pillows but her body moved between them so he could not see what was happening.

"But you were one of the warriors fighting Abrath's army so everyone could escape. If you were expecting me, weren't you worried about us both being killed?" he gulped hoping to distract her.

"Oh TJ" she smiled, turning back towards him, "I didn't know I had you, otherwise I would have made sure we had avoided the battles and your father would have made sure we were on one of the first escape pods to leave."

TJ was relieved to see no sign of her having discovered his hidden comic. He could feel his heart hammering in his chest.

"Was it the same for Aunt Sahara?"

"Oh yes; we only guessed we were pregnant after everyone else had recovered from space sickness and the two of us seemed to get worse. You know long-life space cuisine is really not very appealing second time round" she laughed, looking at her son.

"Yuck" giggled TJ.

Zoe's eyes looked at the star chart again and gradually began to fill with tears.

"Don't cry mum. I know you miss home and dad."

He hugged his mum tight willing her to not cry. She always tried to be so brave but he knew that deep inside she missed Ignea and it was breaking her heart.

"Oh, look at me crying like a baby" she said, wiping the salty tears from her cheeks. "Well you'd best hurry up with that homework I have chores for you to do whilst I do some baking. Aunt Sahara gave me a recipe for her honey cake that you love."

"Chores?" exclaimed TJ in surprise.

Zoe turned as she reached the door.

"Oh yes; chores. You didn't think I'd let you off eating spacebombs and hiding comics under your pillow did you? I am the all-seeing, all-knowing mum so be afraid. Very afraid!"

Giving him her sweetest smile, she pulled the comic out from behind her back and waved it at him before disappearing into the corridor.

TJ sat with his head in his hands, not sure which was the worse punishment; chores or his mum's baking? Sighing deeply he picked up his charting pen and continued on with his homework.

Chapter 4
Ukemi

"It seemed a shame to be indoors on such a lovely day" exclaimed Honas, the martial arts master, as he led the class through the aromatic rosemary hedge that surrounded the academy and out onto the sports field.

Honas was a very small man who exuded an air of calm. The sun glinted on his chestnut brown bald head and the breeze tugged at the wisps of hair that grew just above his ears. His black belt was firmly knotted at the waist of his black suit and the gently slapping of his rush flip-flop sandals could barely be heard above the children's voices.

The children could see, in the shade, beneath the large Maguna tree a huge square of canvass, which had been stretched across foam mats. This was to be their first martial arts lesson and they chattered excitedly as they walked towards the canvass in their crisp, bright white suits.

"This is going to be so great!" TJ said, grinning. "I hope we get to learn some of those flying kicks and punches I've seen the older kids do."

"Oh I hope not. I mean I'm sure that stuff is far too advanced for us beginners and Honas wouldn't let us do something so dangerous. Would he?" asked Chak, visibly turning green at the thought.

Reaching inside his jacket he felt the waistband of his trousers to make sure his secret stash of cocoa drops were held firmly in place. He felt better knowing comfort food would be close at hand in case his sugar levels plummeted.

Honas settled the children down and sat them around the edge of the mat. They were grateful for the shade of the tree as their suits were quite heavy and the direct sunlight would have made the canvass too hot for their poor feet. TJ winked at Jessica as he nudged Chak in the ribs. He had lain awake most of the night, thrilled by the prospect of learning martial arts. He had imagined himself leaping through the air with gravity defying kicks, sweeping over the ranks of Abrath's evil legions. He has been so excited that he had lost count of the times he had climbed out of his sleeping pod to check that his mother had packed his training suit in his bag.

Honas looked at them all with his kindly eyes and a smile creased the leather-brown skin of his face.

"Welcome my little friends to your first martial arts class. I'm sure most of you have been looking forward to this and I'd bet one or two of you couldn't sleep last night" he said, winking knowingly at TJ.

"Martial arts have a very ancient history and its traditions should be treated with the utmost respect at all times. You can never practise martial arts enough and even our greatest warriors live a life of constant practice, always seeking the perfect technique. So you will be following in their footsteps when you practise at home using the schedules I will set you."

Jessica was proudly looking at her pristine suit. She was determined to work hard at martial arts class as it had been her mother's number one subject when she had been student.

"Well, first things first" continued Honas, clasping his wrinkled hands together.

"In the future, a legend will be created. It begins with a wise man called Isaac Newton sitting under an apple tree. While sitting under this tree an apple will fall on his head and he then begins to think why did it happen; why did the apple fall? While deep in thought he will come to the conclusion that every object is subjected to gravity, which is one of the four invisible forces."

"I see. Is that why we stay on the ground and don't float off into space?"

"Yes Chak."

"Or why the moon doesn't spin off into space and why the earth goes around the sun?"

"Basically, that's correct."

At that moment TJ gave Chak a puzzled look.

"How do you know this stuff? " he asked.

"TJ, it's good to read! "Chak replied, looking very smug.

"So why are you teaching this Master Honas?" Chak continued.

"Well, gravity is nature's weakest force but when combined with a kick it can have a devastating effect. The name of this kick is Newton's Gravitational Kick."

"Oh I see" Chak replied.

"You will also need to learn which planets have greater gravity than others so you don't do yourselves any harm by applying more power than what is required."

"That's easy; you just said the bigger and heavier the object the greater the gravity so Jupiter is the largest planet, so it must have the greatest gravity" TJ remarked.

"Very good TJ but that's why the first thing we need to learn is 'ukemi' or break falls. After all, what would be the use of being able to perform fantastic leaping attacks when you can't land properly and end up knocking yourself out? It is important that you know how to fall properly to protect yourself from injury and until you have mastered this we cannot progress on to learning techniques including Newton's Graviational Kick. I will begin by showing a few simple falls and I want you to study how I use my arm to soak up all of the energy of the fall. So please watch carefully."

With those words, he promptly demonstrated a couple of simple falls by tumbling forwards and rolling over in a fast, smooth action. As he landed on the canvass he slapped the mat hard with the palm of his hand and his forearm.

"Now" he said, turning to the class barely out of breath, everyone find a space and try to perform a basic roll. Remember to use your arm to soak up all of the energy as I've just shown you and keep your chin tucked in! We don't want to bump our heads on the floor do we?"

The children spread out into a space as instructed and began trying out a few gentle tumbles with varying degrees of success. Honas moved amongst the class helping those pupils who were struggling.

TJ was finding it a bit of a disappointment and occupied himself by making fun of Chak's rather clumsy attempts. Chak was not feeling very confident and could have done without TJ's remarks. Trying to ignore his friend, Chak decided to put all of his effort into a roll that he was determined to make perfect. Unfortunately he did not look where he was going and managed to bump into Jessica and knocked her flying off of the canvass and on to the grass.

Tears sprang to her eyes as she picked herself up and studied the deep green grass stains on her beautiful, crisp white suit. Glaring at Chak, she noticed TJ in the background rolling around, clutching his sides and laughing hysterically.

Honas' attention was drawn to the commotion and, after instructing the rest of the class to continue practising, he headed over to deal with the problem. Jessica was sobbing and he calmed her by assuring her that the grass stains would not affect her already perfect tumbles. She managed a feeble smile through her tears and Honas persuaded her to continue.

Anticipating a reprimanded for their behaviour, TJ and Chak looked at the master sheepishly.

"I think it might be more useful young man" he said, addressing TJ, "for you to spend a little more time concentrating on your practising than on what other people are doing,"

TJ was relieved. He thought he was going to be in trouble. His current after-class detentions with Kava were almost at an end and he really did not want to start a series of new ones with Honas.

Turning to Chak with an amused look in his eyes Honas said, "I think for someone of your stature it might be an idea for you to allow a little more room for your tumbles."

Also relieved that he was not in trouble, Chak nodded solemnly as Honas turned to walk away.

"Oh, by the way" said the old master, turning back, "the two of you can help me to put away the mats and canvass away after class. I'm sure you won't mind" he grinned as he turned his attention to the other students.

TJ looked at Chak and rolled his eyes. They both decided to apologise to Jessica who had now stopped crying and instead appeared to be smirking as she whispered to Jasmine while pointing at Chak. Jasmine looked at Chak as he approached and tried to stifle a giggle.

"I'm sorry about your suit," said Chak giving the girls a curious look.

"Oh well, these things happen but I must confess I didn't think you would be that scared of Honas" she giggled.

"I wasn't scared of Honas!" protested Chak.

"Well maybe you should look a little closer at your own suit because it certainly looks like you were scared!"

Chak looked down at his jacket then at his back and was horrified to see a dark brown stain on the seat of his trousers. Wondering what it could be he scratched the stain and sniffed his finger much to the disgust of TJ and Jessica. When he decided to lick his finger, Jessica's hand flew to her mouth as she gagged.

"It's okay," said Chak, grinning, "its chocolate" and he explained about his hidden stash of cocoa drops.

The afternoon progressed well and Honas managed to have all the children tumbling over shorter distances at faster speeds. He even had enough time to teach them a few simple kicks and chops to practise at home.

TJ thoroughly enjoyed the class and was in high spirits when Honas instructed the class to return to the academy. He and Chak carefully removed the canvas and folded it for storage. They then began to load the mats on to a nearby hovercart.

"I can't wait until next week's lesson" TJ said, and then, grinning, "I hope we get to learn some flying kicks. You'd best leave your chocolate at home though Chak; it doesn't seem to have done your suit any favours."

"Oh, do you really think we'll have to do flying kicks? You know heights make me dizzy" puffed Chak, feebly lifting a mat.

"How come you always have so many sweets? Your mum must own the sweet booth in Ramon Bazaar!"

"It's because she feels guilty that I haven't got a dad. She tries to make up for it by spoiling me" he replied.

"I haven't got a dad but mum doesn't spoil me. I wish she would. I'm never allowed sweets, she can be really strict sometimes" huffed TJ.

A droning sound began to fill the air, catching TJ and Chak's attention. They dropped the mat they were carrying to the cart and began to search the blue skies above, using their hands to shield their eyes from the sun.

As the sound gradually grew louder, warning sirens began blaring in the distance from the landing station. They continued their search in the skies but could see nothing.

"What do you think it is Chak?" asked TJ

"I don't know" his friend replied, shaking his head while he looked around.

Warning sirens began to blare across the city but the boys stayed put, ignoring the danger and desperate to catch the first glimpse of the incoming aircraft.

"There!" shouted Chak, pointing to a hazy dark shape heading from the west. "It looks like a large ship of some sort and its certainly smoking well,"

A trail of thick dark smoke could be seen behind the shape, which was travelling at quite a speed.

"Well it had better not be Abrath heading this way to pick a fight," said TJ, smirking as he watched the growing shape. "I'd kick his behind from here to Noburu!" he laughed, punching and kicking the air with mock attacks.

"Oh I think a little more training may be needed before you take on Abrath," said Honas appearing from nowhere and startling the boys. "Now come along, surely you heard the sirens; you need to get indoors," said the old man ushering the children towards the academy while searching the skies with his old and tired eyes.

"Yes sir" said TJ, suddenly feeling a little foolish in front of the master.

TJ covered his ears as the droning sound increased to an almost deafening level. He looked at Chak and Honas and could see they too, had covered their ears. Before they could get halfway across the field a large shadow passed over them. Looking up, they could see it was a huge battered cargo vessel. One of the craft's hyperdrive engines was spitting out sparks and flames whilst the other was beginning to splutter. Attached to each side of the cargo vessel were fighter escorts. The smaller ships were attached to the bigger ship by magnetic bindings, which glowed in the sunlight, and they were assisting the larger craft to remain aloft.

Forgetting the potential danger, the two boys and Honas stood and watched the ships descend until they disappeared from view behind the towers of the city's eastern district. The warning sirens continued to blare from the landing station despite those in the city falling silent.

"Wow, that was amazing" gasped TJ. "Did you see how the smaller ships helped that great big one?"

"Yeah!" said Chak still staring off to the east.

"I wonder where it's come from?" said TJ looking at Honas.

"Somewhere none too friendly I should say looking at the damage it has sustained," said Honas. "I'm sure we'll find out soon enough. Now hurry inside with those mats. Kava is waiting for you TJ. He mentioned something about detention, and I think your mother will be waiting for you Chak. Though I doubt she will be pleased to see your suit when she claps eyes on it."

Honas led the two boys into the building as the hover cart followed close behind with a low humming sound.

Chapter 5
Telepathy

On opening her eyes, Jessica found herself floating above the padded floor of the dojo, and higher than she had ever managed before. Feeling herself slowly descending she closed her eyes once more and refocused her mind. Levitation requires total concentration so she pushed all other thoughts from her mind.

She did as Irises had taught her and let herself drift into a deep meditation, relaxing all of her joints and muscles and focussing on directing her mental powers into pushing her body away from the ground.

Everyone had found the first few levitation classes very difficult and it had been several weeks before anyone had managed to levitate. Even then, they had only stayed afloat for matter of seconds.

Feeling herself floating higher, Jessica smiled and released a satisfied sigh.

"See if you can roll over Jessica" said Irises, interrupting her peaceful state of mind.

Not wishing to break her concentration by speaking, Jessica nodded her head slowly. From her cross-legged sitting position she unfolded her legs, stretched her arms before her and gently threw her upper body forward and down so her legs rose in the air in an arc. Feeling herself losing height again, she focussed harder on pushing herself away from the ground.

Irises had told them to imagine the air was liquid and that it was possible to swim through it like water. So Jessica imagined herself swimming and tucked her knees into her chest and used her arms to bring herself back to an upright position.

"Well done Jessica, not bad for a first attempt. Try it again with a little more height this time" suggested Irises.

Pleased at Irises' compliments, she emptied her mind and pushed herself higher. She rolled over in the air once more but this time tried to keep her movements more controlled so she did not feel as though she was flapping around.

Her hair fell away from her head as she rolled upside down and she felt her blood rush to her head making it feel strange. As she righted herself her hair fell back down over her face and tickled her nose. She dared to reach up and brush it aside and felt herself floating downwards as her concentration wavered.

"Well done" praised Irises, "a much more majestic and graceful movement that time. Jessica."

Jessica's cheeks began to redden at Irises' compliments. He did not seem to be paying anyone else any attention and she felt her chest swell with pride.

"Slowly bring yourself down to the ground now everyone" said Irises. "I think you have all practised hard enough for today. I'm very pleased with you all. At our next class I think it will soon be time for you all to begin learning to roll yourselves over in somersaults whilst levitating."

Jessica gently lowered herself to the ground, baffled by Irises plans for the next class. Surely they had all tried rolling forward today. How odd?

Feeling herself coming to rest upon the ground, Jessica opened her eyes and looked about her. The rest of the class was slowly descending. Unfolding her legs, she watched Chak made a rather shaky descent. He seemed to be unable to stop swaying from one side to another and resembled a feather floating down, swishing one way then the other.

He landed on the ground but as he was leaning too far over to the left, he managed to end up sprawled on his left side with his legs still crossed. Irises gently lifted him upright so that he could untie his tangled legs.

Jessica had to smother a giggle as she looked over at TJ. He obviously had cramp in one of his legs and was unable to uncross them. His face was screwed up in discomfort, with his lips pushed out and his eyebrows dancing a frantic jig on his forehead. Irises came to the rescue, helping TJ to uncross his legs and relieve the cramp.

The class began to chatter, excited at the prospect of somersaults in the next class. Jessica tried to explain to her friends that she had already performed somersaults but no one would listen to her.

Irises put his gnarled finger to his whiskery lips and silenced the class. He pointed a figure still hovering high in the air in the corner of the room. It was Brint who was a rather tall and well-built child. He floated in the air deep in meditation unaware that the class had finished. As the children looked on Brint's head rolled back and a rumbling snore broke from his fleshy lips.

The children could not help but giggle at their sleeping classmate. Irises waggled his bushy eyebrows in amusement. The noise of the children woke Brint with a snort. He promptly tumbled to the floor, as his state of 'meditation' was broken. Luckily the padded floor protected him from any serious injury. Straightening himself up him let out a sleepy yawn and rubbed his bleary eyes.

"I think you may have worked a little too hard on your relaxation technique," said Irises smiling. "Might I suggest a good night's sleep before our next levitation class."

"Yes sir" grinned Brint sheepishly before letting out another great yawn.

Irises dismissed the class and the children filed out to collect their belongings before heading home.

Jessica sighed impatiently as she stood with her bag waiting for TJ. He was busy chattering with Chak, each boasting that they had levitated the highest. TJ saw Jessica waiting impatiently so he said goodbye to his friend and went over to her.

"At last! Come on TJ you've been ages" she moaned.

"OK little Miss Happy!" he said, slinging his bag over his shoulder. "What's the hurry anyway? Can't wait to rush home and do your homework?"

"Don't tell me you've forgotten?" she said glaring at him.

"Forgotten what?" he asked a blank expression upon his face.

"We have to meet Mum and Aunt Zoe at the bazaar" she sighed rolling her eyes. "If we do not get a move on we'll be late."

"Oh, shopping," said TJ wearily, "how could I forget?"

"Stop moaning TJ and hurry up" she said, heading towards the door.

"Hey you just try and hold me back," muttered TJ following her out of the Academy, dragging his feet.

Chapter 6
Oh no!

"How long can it take to buy food?" moaned TJ, shifting a heavy bag of groceries from one hand to the other. "Surely we have more than enough here," he said gesturing at the bulging bag.

"That's only fruit and vegetables," replied Jessica watching their mothers looking over the meat hanging on display inside the shop.

The large red-faced butcher was showing Sahara a big joint of meadow bison but she was shaking her head and laughing. Jessica smiled knowing her mother could only dream of affording such a luxurious delicacy. Instead, Sahara was looking through the selection of lizards whilst Zoe inspected the flag goat meat.

TJ gave another sigh and leant against the window to take his weight off of his feet and watched the crowds milling around the busy bazaar.

"This is so boring. I wish we could go to the sweet booth and get some scrumptious lunar liquorice," he said nodding in the direction of the sweet shop.

"You know we're not allowed in there," said Jessica. "Sweets are bad for our teeth and they're expensive. Our mums don't have the money to spare for sweets."

"Looks like Chak's mum doesn't have that problem," said TJ seeing his tubby friend emerge from the sweet shop and with a huge bag clutched in his hand.

TJ turned around to look inside the butcher shop. Their mums seemed to be taking forever. He could see his Aunt Sahara picking out a large gozan lizard and passing it to the butcher.

He turned back to face the street and looked towards the sweet booth to see if Chak was headed their way.

"Chak always shares his sweets," thought TJ, "maybe if I'm lucky he'll pass by before mum comes out of the shop."

Standing on tiptoe he scoured the crowd for his friend. He spotted his bright red hat and saw him passing by two men sitting outside Hinks' Tavern. As TJ looked on a hand shot out from the gap between the tavern and the Maharaja Spice shop and grabbed Chak by the collar. Before Chak could react the hand dragged him into the alley that ran between the two buildings.

"Jessica I think something's happened to Chak" TJ said, looking for a sign of his friend.

"TJ, is that the best excuse you can think of so you can go and talk to him? You just want to help him eat his sweets!" She said glaring at him.

"No!" he protested. "I just saw him dragged into the alleyway. I'm going to see what's going on," he said glancing into the butcher shop. "Here take this bag; I won't be a minute.

"Oh no you don't!" said Jessica taking a step back and refusing the proffered bag. "You're not dumping it on me that easily. Anyway your mum will go mad if she comes out here and finds you missing."

TJ glanced into the shop once more. "You're joking," he snorted. "Aunt Sahara hasn't finished choosing the meat yet let alone begun haggling. Look I won't be a minute. I promise. I just want to make sure he's OK."

He hoisted up the bag and began pushing his way through the crowd towards the alley. Jessica soon lost sight of him amongst the bustling bodies. She looked through the window with an anxious look upon her face. She knew TJ was only worried about his friend but it might have been better if he had told Zoe about it.

Jessica turned back and scanned the crowd but could see no sign of either TJ or Chak. A brief gap appeared through which she could see the two men sitting outside the tavern next to the alley but before she could see any more the crowd closed again.

"Where's your little friend TJ?" said a chirpy voice in her ear making her jump.

"Oh hello" said Jessica, turning around and recognising Jasmine's mother. "He's just up there" she replied pointing in the direction of the alley, "in fact I'd best go and get him I think mum's nearly finished shopping".

"You are a good girl" smiled the plump woman, patting her on the shoulder.

"Great" she thought to herself seeing the woman's portly body squeeze into the entrance of the shop. "She'll keep mum and Aunt Zoe chatting long enough for me to find out what TJ is up to and drag him back before we get into trouble!"

With one last glance into the shop, she grabbed her school bag and headed through the crowd towards the alley. She turned the corner at the tavern and looked into the murky entrance of the passageway. The evening shadows made it look dark and unwelcoming.

The smells wafting out of the spice shop managed to cover up the worst of the stench of the alley and the clatter of dishes from the tavern's kitchens drowned out of the hubbub from the bazaar. She cautiously wandered into the alley, stepping over the litter scattered on the cobbled floor and edged around a huge pile of oak casks that blocked the way.

She froze at the sight before her. TJ and Clark were pinned against the wall by two boys whilst a group of other boys stood around them, jeering. She didn't recognise any of the gang. They were clearly a lot older and the shabby state of their clothes meant they weren't from the Academy.

"No, Fatso" sneered one of the boys as he stepped forward and poked Chak in the stomach. "How about you hand over that big bag of goodies and empty out your pockets?"

"You leave him alone you big bully!" yelled TJ trying to wriggle free.

"Looks like your little friend is going to protect you Fatso" the boy laughed brushing his red hair from his eyes. "Don't think I'd leave you out" he spat at TJ through gritted teeth. "You'll have your chance to empty your pockets too."

"No way! Who do you think you are?" said TJ as he managed to free one arm. He used it to sharply elbow the skinny boy holding him making him howl. The boy doubled over in agony and released TJ's other arm.

Now he was free TJ launched himself at the red-haired boy using the few martial arts techniques he had learnt from Honas. Keeping a firm grasp on his bulging bag of sweets while a spotty lad held his arms in a tight grip, Chak looked on as his friend's fists and legs cut through the air with frightening speed. He thought about struggling but at that very point, the meagre amount of courage he possessed packed its bags and put up the closed sign.

Jessica watched in horror from her hiding place behind a large cask that reeked of cherries. Goodness knows what could happen in the time that it would take her to fetch her mum and Aunt Zoe. She decided to try and rescue her friends herself and only hoped that their mums would be able to find them soon.

Firmly gripping her school bag's long strap she rushed forward and swung it high above her head. The group of boys were taken by surprise as Jessica jumped from her hiding place and hurtled towards them yelling.

The bag struck the nearest boy on his temple with a thump. His eyebrows rose and his eyes rolled upwards until only the whites could be seen. With a sigh his legs buckled underneath him and he slid to the dirty cobbled floor.

Jessica punched her fist in the air in triumph and, spurred on by her success, she ploughed forward swinging her heavy bag even harder. The group tried to scramble out of her way but a very tall lanky boy was unable to move out of her path fast enough and was caught between the legs with a mighty smack from the bag. Jessica smiled to herself as he fell to the floor clutching himself. Tears streamed down his grimy cheeks as he rolled from side to side wailing.

TJ had managed to karate chop the red-haired youth on both arms with mighty blows. The boy curled in a ball hugging his numbed arms to his chest, a high-pitched whining sound coming from his lips.

As Jessica moved forward towards Chak the group of boys backed away from her, ducking underneath the lethal bag. So confident was she that she failed to notice them regrouping behind her. She moved deeper and deeper into the passageway as the spotty lad holding Chak dragged him into a dark dank corner.

She took aim and swung the bag at the spotty boy's head. All of her exertions had made her palms sweaty and the strap slipped from her fingers. The bag flew through the air and struck him hard on the nose with a mighty crack. His hands flew up releasing Chak as blood spurted from his broken nose.

TJ saw an opportunity and gave the boy an almighty kick to the knee forcing him to tumble to the ground. Jessica and TJ both rushed forward and grabbed Chak by the arms. Clasping one of his chubby arms in one hand Jessica retrieved her bag whilst TJ held the other and managed to grab the heavy bag of groceries. His life would not be worth living if he left it behind!

They turned their backs to the corner of the alley and faced towards the entrance of the street. But they had been too slow. Despite several members writhing on the floor in agony, the rest of the gang had regrouped and now had the three youngsters trapped in the corner.

The red-haired boy stepped forward rubbing his arms and sneering. His teeth were crooked and yellow and his breath smelt disgusting. Jessica wrinkled up her nose. TJ held his breath and Chak tried hard not to gag.

"Nice try" he leered glaring at them, "but too bad for you because now not only are you going to give us everything you've got, my friends here are looking for revenge. It seems you've caused them some pain and they just want to be polite and return the compliment!"

The gang behind him cackled and jeered. The children were horrified to see some of them were now wielding sticks as they began to close in.

TJ and Jessica gulped loudly and both could feel Chak shaking between them. There was no escape and Jessica wished she had fetched her mum and Aunt Zoe. She hoped they would walk into the alley and save them but that would be a miracle. TJ's eyes were wide with fear and he felt sweat trickling down his spine. His hands were grasping his friend so tightly that Chak's shaking was making his arm tingle. Jessica's hand was tingling too, and as Chak's shaking increased the sensation spread up her arm and through her body. She stared at the gang who were rapidly closing in. The boy whose nose she had broken stepped forward raising a large piece of wood above his head. Almost in slow motion he swung it downwards towards Jessica who closed her eyes tight waiting for it to thump her on the head. She desperately tried to raise her hands to protect herself but they were paralysed by the tingling sensation.

The wood swung through the air towards Jessica's head. She closed her eyes tighter ready for the blow.

It missed.

The boy's eyes widened in surprise as the wood hit the floor with a thud. The corner where the children had been standing was now empty. The gang were stunned into silence. The red-haired boy moved forward cautiously and waved his hand through the air where the three had been.

Spooked by the children vanishing into thin air the gang ran off towards the street pushing past the two men entering the alley.

Irises and Rathooq froze in their tracks and took a sharp intake of breath. Both closed their eyes and touched their fingertips to their temples. Passers-by stared at the two standing as still as statutes with the breeze tugging at their robes.

Rathooq opened his eyes and turned to Irises.

"What do you think Irises?" he said, as his brow creased with concern.

Before Irises could reply their senses were assaulted once more. Rathooq closed his eyes and touched his temples as the waves of sensation passed over him. They seemed to be coming from the west side of the city.

Irises took a deep cleansing breath and exhaled loudly. Lowering his wrinkled hands he turned his piercing blue gaze to Rathooq.

"I think this is trouble my dear friend. Someone is in difficulty and that second wave tells me trouble is following him or her. No one would have done such a foolish thing in these dark times unless it was a last resort and they had no other option."

"But did you sense how far it was?" said Rathooq, his eyes sparkling with amazement.

"I did" said Irises, scratching his snowy beard, "and no one I know could have managed such a distance. Come Rathooq, we need to hurry back and investigate. I have a very bad feeling about this."

Chapter 7
Where are we?

"I can't see them anywhere," said Sahara standing on tiptoe and scouring the bustling crowd.

"Well Jasmine's mum said only that Jessica was here when she came into the shop. She asked Jessica where TJ was and she said he was somewhere in the direction of the tavern. Jessica was going to fetch him back," said Zoe wringing her hands with worry.

"Let's walk down that way then," said Sahara "they can't have gone far; maybe we'll be able to spot them."

Slinging the bag of gozan lizard over her shoulder Sahara smiled at her friend and began to work her way through the teeming street. She scanned the figures ahead of her for the two youngsters whilst Zoe followed close behind.

"Do you think TJ might have gone to the sweet booth?" asked Sahara over her shoulder.

"Anything is possible," replied Zoe. "That boy certainly has a sweet tooth."

They continued on through the throng of people, passing by the spice shop from which wafted delicious aromatic smells, and the tavern with its rickety tables outside. The two men seated at one of the tables were sorting through their coins to pay the fat, balding innkeeper who stood over them with his hairy arms crossed over his chest.

The women had continued only a short way further when they both stopped suddenly, causing passing shoppers to bump into them. Ignoring the protests around them they lifted their fingertips to their temples and closed their eyes as waves of sensation passed over them.

Opening their eyes the women looked at each other.

"That was close by," said Zoe grabbing Sahara by the sleeve.

Sahara was biting her lip and tears filled her eyes.

"We need to find the children quickly," she said looking back past the now empty tables of the tavern to the butcher shop.

A rapid movement caught her eye and she saw a group of youths dashing from the alley next to the tavern.

She decided to go and investigate the group's suspiciously hasty departure from the alley but just before she and Zoe reached the entrance a second wave washed over them.

"It's in here," said Zoe nodding her head towards the grim looking passageway.

"Come on!" yelled Sahara dragging her friend past the piles of casks and into the cobbled alley.

They searched its length all the way through to the miserable little courtyard that sat behind the tavern. The rusty iron gate was locked fast so no one could have left the alley without passing them.

The women retraced their steps, their hearts pounding in their chests, but they could find nothing. As they turned to leave, something glittering caught Zoe's eye. Bending down she carefully lifted the object from the dirt and turned it over in her palm.

It was a small silver pendant on a broken chain. Zoe pressed a concealed button and the pendant popped open. Inside was a tiny picture of herself and Ignea. Stifling a sob and wiping the tears from her eyes she showed her find to Sahara.

"This is TJ's. I gave it to him when he started at the Academy. It meant so much to him to have a picture of his father that he treasured it. He would never let it out of his sight.

Sahara took her friend in her arms and hugged her close.

"We'll find them. Don't worry Zoe," she said soothing her friend, but inside she was filled with icy cold terror.

〜〜〜〜〜

"Where are we?" said Jessica looking about her.

The three children stood in the shade of a large rocky outcrop. Before them lay mile after mile of sand and sand dunes that stretched as far as the eye could see. The sun shone fiercely from the clear blue sky scorching the barren landscape.

"I guess Chak must know since he brought us here" shrugged TJ, looking at his tubby friend. "So Chak where exactly are we?"

Chak was busy mopping the beads of sweat from his brow. He was taking plenty of time over the task to avoid facing his friends for as long as possible.

"I thought the tingling sensation felt familiar," said Jessica, "but I never guessed it was teleportation. What did you think you were doing?" she asked Chak who was still wiping his brow.

"I...I...I don't know Jessica" he stammered finally looking at her. "All I did was wish really hard that we were someplace else!"

"Well you can just wish us back again," she said glaring at him with blazing eyes.

"I don't think I can," he whimpered. "I'm totally exhausted. In fact I feel a little faint; maybe I need to eat something," he said rummaging in his bag of sweets and popping a purple coloured sweet in his mouth. "Let me rest for a while and maybe we can try later."

Chak lowered himself to the ground and began to make himself as comfortable as was possible on the bare, hard ground.

"Oh great!" snapped Jessica pacing backwards and forwards, "we are in so much trouble TJ; I hope you're happy. All Chak had to do was give those boys the sweets and that would have been that. But oh no, you had to be a hero and save him. Just look where that's got us—the middle of nowhere with no idea how to get home. Our parents are going to be so mad with us and I dread to think what Irises is going to say after he strictly forbade us from using teleportation outside to the school!"

"Me be a hero?" said TJ, staring at Jessica's purple face. "So you weren't being a hero when you came charging in whirling your bag around? Those boys were bullies Jessica and you know it. They wouldn't have been satisfied with a simple bag of sweets and Chak didn't teleport us on purpose did he? It happened because he was scared."

TJ and Jessica stopped arguing as the hairs on the backs of their necks began to prickle. After a few seconds the sensation passed and they both looked at each other in confusion.

"What was that?" said Jessica rubbing her neck.

"I don't know," replied TJ, looking around.

Chak offered no answer as he was gently snoring from his curled up position, totally oblivious to anything.

TJ began studying the rock whilst Jessica searched the desert for any sign of life.

"I think I can see a way up here" he said pointing at the rock's jagged face. "If you can help me up onto the lip of this outcrop I can climb to the top and see what's on the other side. Let's face it Chak can't have teleported us that far from the city."

"What if you fall and hurt yourself?" asked Jessica looking concerned.

"Of course I won't" laughed TJ squeezing her arm. "Doesn't your dad always say I can climb like a burboo monkey every time I scale that big murtar tree in your garden?"

"No" giggled Jessica "he says you look like a burboo monkey."

"Ha ha, very funny" he replied with a smirk, moving towards the jagged lip of the outcrop. "Come on Jessica, give me a hand and I'll be able to reach that bit that hangs down."

Jessica stood in front of TJ with her hands clasped together for her friend to use as a step. He sprang up and launched himself at the drooping part of the rock and scrambled for a firm grip, loosening a shower of spray of debris, which rolled over the lip and rained down on Jessica below. As the small pieces of rock began pelting on her head she rushed to the overhang for shelter, just managing to stop short of stepping on the slumbering Chak.

She looked down at him and suddenly felt guilty for losing her temper. She knew Chak hadn't teleported them on purpose but she was afraid their parents wouldn't be able to find them. In fact if she was to be honest she was scared to death.

She drew in a deep breath and sighed loudly. A sour stench filled her nostrils and she began to move around, sniffing. She sniffed Chak who though not smelling too fresh certainly was not responsible for the awful smell. After a few minutes of sniffing she began to realise her hands felt a bit sticky. Looking down she could see that they were covered in a bright green filthy muck. The stink was now so bad it made her eyes water.

"Argh!" she cried trying to rub it off on the rock. "Ooh TJ you wait till you get back. I'm going to kill you!" she seethed.

Looking she could see his bright green footprints leading from a pile of lizard droppings to where she had helped lift him up.

"Here, use this to wipe it off," said a strange voice startling her.

CꞋꞋꞋꞋꞋꞋꞋ

TJ slowed hoisted himself up and began climbing up the rock face. It was not too steep and there were plenty of places on which to get a grip with his hands and feet. The hardest part of the climb was the sun beating down which burned his head and made the rock hot to touch.

He paused and reached for his scarf to wrap around his head for protection. As his fingers loosened the knot at his throat he suddenly realised his small chain and locket were missing.

A sob escaped from his lips as frantically searched his clothing for it with one hand whilst clinging on to the rock with the other.

It was gone. TJ was devastated.

With a heavy heart he tied the scarf on his head and carried on climbing. His eyes kept filling with tears and he had to keep brushing them away with the back of his dusty hand.

His arms and legs were heavy and weary as he finally reached the top of the rock. Dust covered his clothes and shoes and his hands stung where the sharp edges of the rock had made small scratches and cuts.

TJ pulled himself up so he could stand on the top of the rock and look around him. Behind were the dunes they had seen from the outcrop below. In front was more desert stretching for mile after mile after sandy mile. He squinted hard at the horizon whilst shielding his eyes from the bright, fierce sun. A tiny shape could be seen in the distance. It was little more than a smudge on the horizon. He waited patiently and watched the shape. It appeared to move. As the sun began its descent in the western sky, slowly but surely the smudge began to take shape.

Piece by piece the lengthening shape of a line of camels became clearer to TJ's straining eyes. It was a trade caravan from one of the cities. If they were lucky it might be heading to Neo-Anapious. If not, it had to be heading somewhere that would be better than where they were now.

It was still a very long way off and TJ guessed they were miles away; too far to pass before dark. He would climb back up at first light and check their position. Attracting their attention would be difficult but TJ was confident that between the three of them they would think of something.

As he turned to climb back down something on his left caught his attention. The slowly reddening glow of the setting sun was being reflected by something far off in the distance of the darkening eastern sky. TJ once more screwed his eyes tight and squinted for a better view. He could barely make out the outline of some kind of structure but it resembled no building of Neo-Anapious.

Shrugging his shoulders he surveyed the looming darkness of the sky and decided he had best make the most of the last of the light to climb back down to Jessica. As he scrambled down the rock face his stomach let out a loud protest. He had not eaten since lunchtime at the Academy and he suddenly realised how hungry he was.

His limbs ached as he reached the lip of the outcrop and his hands were stinging. He eased himself back over the lip, feeling his legs swinging in the air. He heard a movement below and could no longer hear Chak snoring.

"Oh no" thought TJ, "I hope Chak hasn't found the fruit in the shopping bag and scoffed the lot!"

The second his scratched fingers let go of the rock to drop to the floor a pair of strong hands grasped his waist.

Chapter 8
The Forbidden Zone

Rathooq paced up and down the length of Irises'
study. The walls were lined with shelves heaving
with ancient books, and papers lay scattered
on the untidy desk. Irises stood looking out the
window, stroking his beard whilst totally lost in in
his thoughts.

Zoe and Sahara sat holding hands on the large
dusty couch that filled one corner of the cluttered
room. Their puffy red eyes stared into space.

Irises' faithful servant, Gregor, broke the
silence by ushering in a tall, willowy woman with
a shock of orange hair. She looked at each person
in the room in turn and finally rested her jade
green eyes on Irises.

"Where's Chak, Irises?" she asked with fear
tingeing her voice.

"I'm sorry Grace, we don't know for sure,"
replied Irises, leading to her a seat as her eyes
filled with tears. "All we do know" he continued,
"is that he is with TJ and Jessica. It seems they

are somewhere close to the forbidden zone in the south."

"Oh my, in the forbidden zone!" she gasped clenching her fists in her lap.

"Near, not in Grace. At least we can be thankful for that" Irises replied, smiling wearily.

"But I don't understand; how on Earth did they get there?" she said looking at the others. "That's hundreds of miles from the city. Oh my poor baby. He'll waste away to skin and bones out there," she cried wringing her hands.

"It would seem they teleported there. I know," said Irises raising his hand before she could interrupt, "that it is a very long way to teleport and I'm not sure which of the three managed it. I doubt that they will have the strength for quite some time to perform such a feat again."

"Why would they have done that?" asked Zoe. "They know teleportation is forbidden outside of the Academy."

"Fear" replied Rathooq, perching on the edge of the desk. "They were afraid of something and I guess natural instinct took over. I don't think it was intentional."

"Then who was it that followed them?" asked Zoe.

"Followed them!" screeched Grace, glaring at Irises. "My little angel is in danger? Irises what is going on?"

"I don't know," answered Irises, pinching the bridge of his nose between his thumb and forefinger. "I've tried to contact them using telepathy. They don't know about their telepathic skills yet but even so it shouldn't be too difficult to reach them. I think there must be some kind of interference from the forbidden zone which is preventing me from getting through."

"But what are we going to do?" exclaimed Grace wringing her hands. "We can't just leave them out there! Oh my poor little lamb lost out there in that wilderness."

"A team of warriors are forming to head out from the city within the hour. Rathooq will be in charge. It will take quite a while for them to get there but with any luck, the children will have sought out some shelter," said Irises.

"Why can't the warriors simply teleport there? It would be far quicker." Grace's voice was rising and becoming hysterical.

"My dear Grace, none of our warriors can teleport such a range and even if they could, teleportation is forbidden. There are no exceptions."

"But we are light years away from Abrath. Surely it wouldn't do any harm. Please Irises" begged Grace with pleading eyes.

"Abrath has a vast network of spies and sympathisers, Grace. It is even possible that there are some here on Earth, too. We just cannot risk it."

"That can't be true" she scoffed while looking at the others.

"I'm afraid it is very true. Today I have received communications from Andromeda. My reliable sources there have warned me not to underestimate Abrath's abilities to spread his evil tentacles everywhere. They provided information and evidence that some of the residents of Neo-Anapacious cannot be trusted."

Rathooq rose to his feet and looked at Irises.

"It's time for me to go. I need to fetch my battle armour before meeting the others."

Zoe and Sahara rose to their feet as well.

"We want to go," they said in unison.

"Me too" said Grace, jumping up from the seat.

"I will need you all here" replied Irises. "The children might teleport back home in which case you will be required here to protect them in case trouble follows them. I know I can rely on my two fiercest warriors" he smiled looking at Zoe and Sahara with affection. "And of course Chak will no doubt need to be nurtured back to full strength and only you could do that" he smiled at Grace despite the fact he found her a rather hysterical individual.

Rathooq kissed Sahara and said farewell to the others. He gave Zoe's hand a squeeze and promised to find the children.

Chapter 9
Who are they?

The more TJ struggled to break free, the tighter the bands that pinned his arms to his sides became.

"It's no use TJ," whispered Jessica "they're kinetic bands you won't be able to loosen them."

"Well at least I'm trying" he hissed back, looking at Chak who sat in the corner sobbing and sniffing as the bands squeezed his plump frame.

"Leave him alone, he cannot help being scared. We need to use some brainpower and think our way out of this."

With a huge sigh, TJ gave up his struggle and sat down with a thud on the hard dusty floor under the rocky outcrop.

"Who do you think they are Jessica?" he asked in a hushed voice. "What would they want with three lost kids? Maybe they're gonna ask our parents for ransom money!"

"Don't be ridiculous TJ. What on Earth would our parents pay a ransom demand with? Fresh air? I don't know what they are up to," she said, looking at the two scruffy men standing outside talking, "but I'll bet whatever it is its no good." She winced as the bands began to pinch.

"Chak" she whispered "if we shuffle together do you think you can try and teleport us again?"

"No" he blubbed, "I can't feel my arms any more. I'll bet they've injected something evil into me so my arms become paralysed. How will I be able to eat with no arms?" he wailed. "That's if I live long enough. I haven't eaten for ages and I'm feeling very faint. Maybe I'm dying!"

"For goodness sake" hissed Jessica, "pull yourself together. It takes more than a couple of hours without food to die of starvation! Your arms are only numb because the bands are cutting off your circulation. Now if we shuffle together can you teleport us back?"

"No" he whined. "I'm too exhausted."

"But you were asleep for ages."

"Yes I know but my precious sleep was disturbed. Do you know how terrifying it was to wake up and find my arms bound? In my delicate condition I could have had a heart attack."

"Oh don't be so ridiculous" she snapped glaring at him "there's nothing wrong with you other than being a lazy bones and eating too many sweets."

"Oh, don't talk about food" he moaned, "I'm starving."

"Me too" added TJ, feeling his stomach gurgle.

"Oh for goodness sake" said Jessica with a sigh of exasperation. "Can the two of you just try not to think of your stomachs for a change.   Shhhh! Look one's coming over."

The two men had stopped talking and the taller one was headed towards the children. He was tall and lean with closely shaved hair and a vivid scar that was conspicuous because it resembled the shape of a scarab, a beetle. His clothes were well worn and grubby and his boots were dirty and scuffed.

"Who are you and what do you want?" demanded TJ as the man drew closer to them.

"Oh you don't need to know who I am little fella" the man grinned "and as to what I want. Well" he said scratching the stubble on his chin "I think I'd be happy to settle for the nice sum of money I'm gonna get for you. It seems there's someone very keen to make your acquaintance."

"Well I'm not too keen to make theirs," said TJ, sticking out his chin out stubbornly.

"Well let's look at it this way," said the man, still smiling. "Seeing as you're all tied up I guess you don't really have much choice in the matter. Now that's enough yapping. On your feet, it's nearly time for us to be making a move."

"Where to?" asked Jessica rising to her feet.

"No need to concern yourself little miss. All you kiddies need to do is cause me no trouble. On your feet you" he said, shoving Chak with the toe of his boot.

"Ouch" cried Chak struggling to his feet.

"No need to be a drama queen" said the man. "I barely touched you. Now shuffle together like good little kids. I think we've had enough talking for now so you best keep those little lips buttoned. You understand?"

All three children nodded in silence and moved together as instructed. The man carefully threaded a larger kinetic band through the bands that tied each of them, linking them together in a chain.

He then headed back outside to join his partner, a short, skinny man with narrow features who with his beady eyes cast angry glances in the direction of the children. On his hand were the ancient markings of the Tupai tribe. Jessica thought to herself that the markings were from the Krako period. That was how she thought of the two men; Scarab because of the scar and Tupai because of those natural markings. Both men gave her the creeps.

The two men surveyed the surrounding landscape that was now coloured red by the rapidly setting sun. A chilly breeze blew around the rock, ruffling their clothes and hair and the sad, lonely howl of a desert fox called out across the sands.

Jessica was so scared. They were miles from home and there was no sign that their parents were close to finding them. She did not want the others to see how frightened she was and swallowed down her unshed tears. She whispered over her shoulder to TJ to ask what he had seen from the top of the rock.

TJ described the distant caravan and how he had hoped they might have attracted its attention in the morning. He also told her about the structure that he had seen glinting on the horizon. Jessica wracked her brain but could shed no light on what it might be.

"Maybe if one of us could escape and get to the caravan at first light we can get help" she suggested.

"I don't think there's any way we are going to be able to break free of these bindings," said TJ miserably shrugging at the bands.

"I think you're right" Jessica replied with a sigh, staring at the men.

The sun had now completely disappeared below the horizon leaving just a red glow in the western sky. With the creeping darkness came the cold and the children found themselves shivering. They were wearing light summer clothes that offered little or no protection from the cold of nights in the desert.

The two men suddenly stopped talking and stood frozen for a few moments as if lost in thought. They then turned back to the children and began checking the bindings. Jessica decided to try once more to get some information from them.

"Where are you taking us?" she asked, wriggling as the shorter man pulled the bindings tighter.

"If you don't shut up" said Tupai, glaring at her "I'll cut your tongue out."

He laughed as he pulled out a short blade from his pocket and waved it under her nose. She immediately closed her mouth, her face reddening with fury.

Chak stood silently shivering in the chill night air with his head bowed as the taller man tightened the knots of the bindings. TJ gave the men his meanest stare, which much to his disappointment had no effect on either of them.

The taller man with the scar took hold of the end of the kinetic line that fastened the children together in a single line and led them outside. No longer under the shelter of the rocky outcrop, the wind whipped around them, blowing sand in their faces and stinging their eyes.

The shorter man followed behind the children carrying Jessica's school bag and the bag of groceries in one hand. With the other hand he grabbed TJ by the shoulder. Before TJ could react and shake off the man's hand he felt the familiar tingling sensation. He only prayed that this time Chak would leave Scarab and Tupai behind.

CHAPTER 10

................?

Jessica opened her eyes as the last of the tingling sensations ebbed away from her body. She could feel her hair standing on end from the static of teleportation but the kinetic bands around her arms prevented her from reaching up to tidy her hair. Frustrated she sighed loudly and looked grimly about her through her wild tressels covering her face.

The children had been teleported aboard some kind of vessel. Looking around she could see they were in an empty storage area. The floor was dirty and greasy and the air was tainted with a metallic smell.

She was upset to see that Scarab and Tupai were still with them. TJ looked over at her and his eyes filled with disappointment. Chak stood quivering with his eyes shut tight.

Scarab still held the end of the kinetic line and he led the children towards one of the doors of the bay. He pressed his hand against a panel next to the doorframe. They heard a beeping sound and the door slid open.

The children were led out into a cluttered corridor. One of the wall panels was missing and a tangle of wires hung out like a collection of coloured worms. Their feet clattered on the metal flooring as they were taken along several long corridors. Finally they stopped before another set of doors. Scarab pressed his hand against the panel and the doors swished open to reveal some living quarters.

The room was fairly sparsely furnished, containing only four tatty looking sleeping pods, a battered table and four chipped and worn chairs. They were ushered into the room by the men and Tupai closed the doors by pressing his palm against the panel inside the room.

The two men removed the kinetic bands from the children who immediately began to rub their arms vigorously to restore some blood circulation into limbs that were numb from the pressure of their bindings.

"Here we are kiddies," said Scarab. "Make yourselves at home. I don't want any trouble so you behave and I'll make sure you get something to eat. But try my patience and I'll leave you hungry."

The mention of food made Chak's mouth water and his stomach growled loudly. TJ and Jessica glared at him but he just smiled back weakly.

"It seems our little friend here is in need of nourishment" Scarab said with a laugh, "though

I'm sure a couple of day's starvation would do him no harm. I'll be back soon to check on you and remember," looking at each one in turn, "I don't want any trouble. Understand?"

The three children nodded wearily too tired and hungry to speak. Tupai placed the grocery bag and Jessica's school bag on the table then stepped through the door into the corridor. Scarab followed him out of the room and touched the control panel to close the doors.

The children were alone.

Chak immediately burst into floods of tears. Jessica was too tired to keep putting on a brave face and tears trickled down her cheeks, too. She looked over and saw TJ was wearing his brave face; the one she had seen many times when he was in trouble.

"Come on" she sniffed with a wobbly smile "its no use us crying. I'm sure warriors aren't supposed to cry."

TJ smiled back.

"Yeah, you're right Jess. Come on Chak, that's enough. Stop crying or you'll flood the room."

Chak began to howl even louder. Big fat tears rolled down his shiny red cheeks and dropped from his wobbling chin. TJ went over to him and touched his shoulder.

"Hey Chak. It's not that bad," he said before pausing. "Ok, so its not looking too good either but hey! I'm here and so is Jessica. We're not going to let them get away with this are we?"

Chak's shoulders trembled as he sobbed. Slowly he shook his head from side to side.

"That's the spirit," said TJ grinning "now turn off the waterfall. There can't possibly be any more liquid left inside of you!"

Chak howled and sobbed even harder. TJ looked at Jessica and shrugged his shoulders.

"What is it Chak?" he said turning back to his blubbering friend.

"I can't tell you" he gulped.

"Why not?" asked TJ, looking puzzled.

Chak looked at Jessica with his puffy red eyes then turned back to TJ.

"Because of her" he whispered, jerking his head towards Jessica.

"Why?" asked TJ who was becoming more baffled by his friend's behaviour.

"It's embarrassing."

"OK— look, whisper it in my ear. Jessica won't listen will you?"

"Oh don't mind me" she huffed, "I would step out into the corridor to give you some privacy except that our jailers seem to have locked the door. So inconsiderate I know" she drawled sarcastically. "But I'll tell you what; I'll stick my fingers in my ears and you just get it off your chest Chak."

Glaring at the two boys she promptly stuck her fingers in her ears and began singing.

"La la la la la la la..."

TJ rolled his eyes. This was all he needed. He was now locked in a room with a girl in a stroppy mood and a hysterical hypochondriac. Sighing loudly, he looked at Chak.

"OK Chak she can't hear you now so what is it?"

"La la la" went Jessica, sitting herself on one of the chairs and swinging her legs.

Happy that she could not hear, Chak leant closer to TJ and whispered in his ear.

"You'll have to say it a bit louder Chak. I can't hear you over Jessica's noise."

Again Chak whispered but TJ just shook his head.

"Look Chak you need to speak up. Jessica seems determined to drown out the world."

"La la la la la"

Jessica paused to suck in a deep breath then continued louder than before.

"LA LA LA LA LA....."

Chak was now going purple in the face with frustration.

"I NEED TO USE THE BATHROOM!" he yelled, clutching his belly and crossing his legs.

Jessica stopped chanting and pulled her fingers from her ears.

"If you don't want me to hear things," she snapped "it might be better if you don't shout them out."

"But you were making too much noise" he whined before he resumed sobbing.

"There must be a control panel in the room somewhere that opens the bathroom door," said

Jessica. "You look over there TJ, and I'll search over here."

The two children began searching for the panel. Their search became more frantic as the volume of Chak's howling increased. Jessica searched the back wall of the cabin where she found a small row of buttons with strange symbols on them. She called TJ over and they both stared at them.

"What do you think they are?" asked Jessica.

"I don't know," replied TJ, shrugging his shoulders.

"Oooh hurry up!" howled Chak, jiggling about.

"We'll just have to press them and see," said Jessica.

Carefully she pressed the first button and immediately cold, icy blasts of air shot out from the vents in the ceiling.

"Argh!" cried the children, shivering.

"Not that one then" said Jessica, quickly jabbing the button again to turn it off."

Chak was now clenching his eyes shut and biting his lip. Jessica pressed the next button and the room was filled with soft gentle music played over the sound of waves washing against a shore. An illuminated panel had appeared next to the button and as she moved her hand over it the sound of waves was replaced with bird song and a babbling brook.

"Turn it off!" pleaded Chak through gritted teeth unable to bear the sound of running water.

TJ and Jessica could not help but giggle. She pressed the button again and silence fell around them. Silence that is except for Chak's desperate whimpering. With only two more buttons to try Jessica pressed the third one.

The room immediately went pitch black. Jessica felt something brush against her arm and she jumped away screaming. TJ burst out laughing.

"Scaredy cat!" he giggled, "You're so easy to scare. OK let's turn the lights back on."

"Look what you've done. I can't find the buttons," said Jessica frantically scrabbling at the wall.

"But you had your finger right on the button" said TJ.

"Yes I did" Jessica replied shortly; "until some bright spark thought it would be funny to make me jump."

"Oooooh hurry!" whined Chak from the inky blackness of the room. "I'm afraid of the dark."

"It's OK I think I've found it," said Jessica.

The babbling brook sound surrounded them in the darkness. They could hear the noise of it splashing and gurgling as gentle soothing music played.

Chak began sobbing loudly and begged Jessica to turn it off. TJ was laughing so hard he stumbled and knocked into Jessica.

"TJ get off!" she snapped crossly. "Oh no I've lost the buttons again."

"It's OK" giggled TJ "I've found them. Here we go....."

Icy blasts shot out of the air vents, freezing the children. Jessica could feel her hair blowing everywhere.

"Great" she thought "between this and the teleportation, my hair's going to be a wild thing. Oh I wish I'd tied it up this morning."

She began grabbing at her hair to try and keep it under control whilst she yelled at TJ. Somehow he had found the volume control and the brook was babbling at full blast.

Jessica gave up trying to tame her mane of hair and groped around blindly for TJ. She found him and tried to push him away from the buttons but he grabbed her as he stumbled and the pair of them tumbled to the ground. Chak was now wailing and moaning like a wild animal.

A shaft of bright light suddenly fell across the children.

"What the ...." Exclaimed Scarab who was standing in the open doorway staring at the chaotic scene before him.

Chak lay writhing on the floor clutching his belly. His face was purple and shiny with sweat. Jessica and TJ lay in a tangled heap. A bright red egg shape was beginning to appear on his forehead where he had bumped it again the wall and Jessica was peering through the tangles of unruly hair that fell across her face.

"I thought I told you I didn't want any trouble," yelled Scarab over the noise of the babbling brook.

He strode into the room, placed a tray of food on the table and turned his attention to the buttons on the wall. As he pressed the buttons the music stopped playing, the vents stopped pumping freezing air into the room, and the lights came back on.

"What's wrong with him?" he asked, pointing at Chak.

"Erm, well...." began TJ.

"He needs the bathroom" interrupted Jessica, getting to her feet and brushing the dust from her clothes. "We were trying to find the button for the bathroom but we didn't understand the symbols on them."

"You can't understand Elyon?" he said looking at them in surprise. "I can't believe they don't teach you it at school."

Shaking his head, Scarab pressed the last button—the one that had not been tried—and immediately a panel in the wall slid back silently to reveal a compact but functional bathroom.

Before anyone could speak Chak barged past them and dived into the room, frantically fumbling with the fastenings of his trousers.

"Hey you! You might want to press the button on the wall there" said Scarab pointing with his bony finger. "I don't know about your friends but I certainly don't want to watch you."

Chak's head jerked up and he jabbed at the button on the bathroom wall. The panel closed silently leaving TJ and Jessica alone with Scarab

"I brought you some food," said the man, nodding at the tray. "There's only water to drink but I guess you can't afford to be too fussy right now."

"Where is this ship going?" asked Jessica.

"Told you before. No need for you to be concerned about that" Scarab replied as he headed towards the door. "I suggest you guys eat some food and get some sleep."

"Well can't you at least tell us how long we'll be stuck in here? Jessica pleaded.

"Not too long, just a couple of days" he said "but believe you and me, this place will seem like a palace compared to where you're going."

The craft suddenly shuddered and the faint whining sound of the engines increased.

"What was that?" asked Jessica, her eyes opening in fear.

Scarab chuckled to himself before answering.

"I guess young miss you're not used to space travel. That's the hyperdrive engines kicking in sweetie; nothing for you to worry about."

"But...."

Scarab held his hand out before she could say anything more.

"That's enough questions," he said.

He stepped out into the corridor and the doors slid shut behind him.

The door to the bathroom slid open and Chak stepped back into the room. A disgusting smell followed him and TJ quickly pressed the button to close the door.

"Ah that's better," said Chak, sighing.

TJ and Jessica just glared at him.

"Ooh food!" he said his eyes lighting up. "Great I'm starving," he said heading towards the tray, rubbing his hands together.

The children sat around the table and looked at the plates of colourless food.

"I think I've lost my appetite," said Jessica pushing her plate away.

"Oh can I have it?" asked Chak his piggy little fingers already reaching for the food.

"Hey I want it," said TJ looking disgruntled, "I'm hungry, too."

"Just share it!" snapped Jessica.

The boys looked at each other and rolled their eyes. They quietly tucked into their own food leaving Jessica's congealing on its plate. They would wait until she had calmed down a bit before fighting over it.

"What do you reckon is in these?" asked Jessica pointing to some foil packets on the tray.

TJ picked one up and opened it.

"Looks like some kind of biscuit" he said as he removed it from the packaging and bit into it. "Bit dry but not bad. Here, try it."

Jessica broke off a piece to try and passed the rest to Chak. TJ was right. It was a bit dry but the taste was not unpleasant. She had an idea.

"Why don't we save these," she suggested. "If we do manage to escape when we get to where they're taking us we'll need food."

"But those are for dessert!" exclaimed Chak looking horrified.

"Jessica's right, Chak. Let's save them for an emergency. Look you have Jessica's food—I'm full up" he said, pushing her plate towards his friend.

Chak sat sulking with his bottom lip poking out.

"But mum always gives me dessert" he whined.

Jessica stared at him in disbelief. TJ could sense a row brewing and decided to try and keep the peace.

"But think how proud she'll be of her little warrior when she finds out what a big sacrifice you've made to help our escape plan."

Chak put a fork full of food in his mouth and chewed whilst thinking about it.

"OK" he said, eventually picking up Jessica's plate and slopping its contents on top of his own.

Jessica wrinkled her nose in disgust and poured herself a beaker of water.

"I'll put them in with the fruit" she said picking up the biscuits and putting them into the grocery bag.

The children finished their meal and stacked the dishes on the tray. Jessica ventured into the bathroom and was relieved to find Chak's odour had gone. Looking in the mirror she was horrified to see what a mess she looked. Her hair was sticking out in all directions and her clothes were grubby and wrinkled. Carefully she combed her hair with her fingers and washed the grime from her face and hands.

Snores welcomed her back into the room and she was disgusted that neither of the boys had bothered about washing before going to bed. Climbing into one of the empty sleeping pods, she thumped the lumpy pillow into shape and pulled the thermo blanket over herself. Tiredness soon overtook her and she quickly fell into a restless sleep.

Jessica was glad to leave the spaceship. She had suffered from space sickness and had spent the entire week of their journey huddled in her sleeping pod feeling very sorry for herself. The food they had been served daily had not improved her appetite and her clothes had begun to hang from her frame as she had lost some weight.

The boys had seemed unaffected and their appetite remained as rampant as ever. Several times she had dragged herself out of the sleeping pod to take the foil wrapped biscuits away to store them in the grocery bag before the boys could devour them.

In all the time they had been on the spaceship there had been no sign of Tupai. Scarab had been the only one to visit them whilst they were locked in their cabin and that was only to bring them food. He had little to say to the children but he had checked on Jessica and tried to get her to eat.

They had not been teleported this time to the planet's surface. Instead, the craft had landed and the children had been bound and blindfolded before being led off the ship. Strange sounds swamped them as they entered what Jessica guessed must have be a landing station. She could hear the sound of heavy machinery and the murmur of conversations in some foreign dialect. The air tasted dusty and gritty and smelt earthy.

She recognised Tupai's voice talking in the strange language to another. He seemed to be getting quite aggressive with whomever he was talking. Jessica was pushed forward roughly and, unable to raise her hands to protect herself she bumped into someone in front of her.

"Ouch!" yelled Chak.

"Sorry" exclaimed Jessica "Someone pushed me."

"Well be a bit more careful!" he snapped.

Before she could reply they were all shoved forward and led further into the building. The ground was slowly becoming more uneven and their blindfolds made it difficult for the children. Chak fell over several times and had to be hauled back to his feet.

The group came to a halt and the men removed the blindfolds from the children but left their arms bound. Chak was sobbing and Jessica could see a nasty graze on his forehead. It must have happened during one of his tumbles. Tupai looked over and gave her a sickly grin. She glared back at him defiantly, determined not to show how afraid she was.

They were standing in a dark, rocky corridor that was lit at intervals by flickering lamps. The air felt damp and moist and the downward sloping floor was slick with water that trickled down the walls and dripped from the ceiling. As the group moved off again, a gentle breeze blew from behind them and Jessica guessed they were being let further underground.

They could hear hammering noises ahead and the occasional loud rumble that shook the floor. A foul smell wafted from the direction of the sounds that caused the children to wrinkle their noses in disgust.

Scarab led the way down the corridor that began to slowly widen as the noise level increased. The children followed in single file behind him, struggling to stay upright as they lost their footing on the slippery floor. Tupai brought up the rear, still carrying Jessica's bag and the heavy grocery bag. Jessica could hear him cursing under his breath as he swapped the heavier one from one hand to the other.

After a while the corridor opened out into a vast cavern hundreds of feet high. The corridor came out halfway up the side of the cavern and was only accessible by a set of stone steps cut into the side of the rocky wall.

The three children stared at the sight below them. On the far side of the cavern at ground level was a huge black opening. They could barely see anything. The few flickering lamps scarcely penetrated the inky blackness. A loud rumbling sound came from the darkness of the opening and slowly, a huge form emerged from its depths.

The children gasped and recoiled in horror as a large beast took shape in the entrance of the opening. It was a colossus of a dinosaur-like beast with a large head, and a wide mouth full of fearsome looking teeth. Its stocky body stood on four solid legs, each of which TJ guessed to be as tall as a man. Along its back rose triangular spines that continued all the way down to the fork-like ending of its long tail.

A huge chain was wrapped around the beast's neck and a hefty looking harness was shackled to its shoulders. As it moved forward into the cavern, an immense cart appeared from the gloom behind it. The cart rumbled into the cavern on two giant wheels and was full of shiny looking rocks.

They watched as the beast pulled the heavy cart whilst being shepherded by a fat, ugly man dressed in dusty red overalls. He was carrying a long pole at the end of which was a vicious looking prod. Each time he poked the animal with the pole it made a loud zapping noise and the animal gave a low growl.

The cavern below then became a hive of activity. More men in red overalls carrying prods supervised a group of beings that were no taller than the children. Each had a shock of tangled white hair and their pale bodies glinted with sweat. They were dressed in a few measly rags, barefoot and their legs were shackled with heavy looking manacles.

The men in overalls herded the pale beings toward the cart to unload the shiny rocks that were then carried across the cavern and loaded on to a train of smaller carts waiting in the mouth of a gloomy smaller tunnel, to the left of where the children were standing.

Scarab led the way for the children to follow him down the crumbling dusty stairs with Tupai close behind them. Their descent was slow as the stairs were narrow and the children were unable to steady themselves because of their bound arms. They had walked a considerable distance since leaving the ship and their legs had begun to feel like lead. Chak was flagging behind TJ and Jessica and was grizzling loudly. Tupai prodded him roughly in the back to hurry him up.

At ground level the noise was almost deafening. The children stared about them in fear and wonder. The pale beings had almost finished emptying the huge cart of its shiny looking black rocks while the ominous rumble from the black opening signalled the imminent arrival of another. The men with the prods began yelling and jabbing the poor things. The prods made zapping noises as they touched their sweaty bodies making them whimper and yelp.

Jessica began to walk towards them, determined to give them a piece of her mind but Scarab grabbed her by the collar and drew her back into line. Unable to watch such cruel treatment, she turned away in disgust and followed TJ and Chak as they were led along the edge of the cavern and into another dark corridor. This one was much larger than the one they had been in before. It too was lit with spluttering torches of flame and the ground was very dusty and worn. The corridor snaked in twists and turns, with other corridors leading from it in different directions.

Soon they felt totally disorientated as Scarab led them deeper into the labyrinth of tunnels and the sounds from the main cavern behind them grew fainter. Jessica and the boys were very tired but each time she slowed, Tupai kept pushing her and hurrying her along.

Eventually they were led into a cavern that housed some of the beasts that pulled the carts. There were about twenty of the creatures, each asleep in a stall. The chains on their necks were attached to huge metal rings set into the wall. The smell of them was almost overpowering. Chak squeaked in fear as they were pushed into the cavern and he could no longer be sure whether he was crying or his eyes were watering from the stench.

They were led to an empty stall at the rear of the cave where the men chained them to a metal ring using shackles similar to those worn by the pale beings. Too tired to put up any resistance, the children sat meekly as the men removed their kinetic bands and filled the stall with straw.

"Told you that the quarters on the ship would be a palace compared to this, didn't I?" chuckled Scarab, sprinkling handfuls of straw around.

"Oh I don't know. It seems to have all the comforts of home," said TJ sarcastically.

Tupai fetched a bucket of water from the far side of the cave. A metal mug was attached to the bucket's handle for them to drink from. TJ was gasping for a drink but stubbornly refused to touch the water. He would wait until the men had gone. Jessica felt exactly the same way.

Chak, on the other hand threw all dignity to the wind and with his two hands leading the way, plunged his head straight in the bucket and took noisy gulps of the water. The two men looked at him in disgust whilst TJ and Jessica stared at him in disbelief. Scarab handed Jessica a small rough sack. She looked inside and saw hunks of grey bread that did not look particularly appetising. She closed the bag and glared at the man.

Chak had now taken his fill of water and wiped his hand across his fleshy lips. Just when Jessica thought he could not possibly disgust her any more, he clutched his ample belly and burped loudly. The sound reverberated around the cave, disturbing the sleeping beasts. TJ and Jessica glared at Chak who just grinned back at them.

"Where are we?" said Jessica addressing the men

Once again Tupai remained silent, letting Scarab do all of the talking.

"I thought you were a bright lassie" he said, "but obviously I was wrong. It's no good keep asking me because I am not going to tell you. This is where we say goodbye little kiddies. We've delivered the goods and now we're gonna collect our big fat reward. You have yourselves a fun time and watch out for your roommates here," nodding towards the sleeping animals. "Those beauties have been known to rip a man's arm off for no reason, so you watch out!" At this bit of news, Tupai let out a wheezing laugh.

"Why would anyone pay you a reward for a couple of kids?" asked TJ.

"Who knows and who cares" replied Scarab with a chuckle. "So long as they pay up, that's all I care about. Sweet dreams kiddies."

The two men headed out of the cave leaving the children alone with the sleeping animals. Chak has pressed himself into the corner and was staring at the animals with fearful eyes.

Jessica was too exhausted to cry. Silently she shared out the bread. It tasted disgusting but she knew she needed to eat something to keep her strength up. TJ shared out some of the fruit from the grocery bag that was beginning to over-ripen. Despite Chak having stuck his head in it earlier, she drank a cup of water. . She was too tired to care.

TJ also ate his bread in silence before piling up some hay to make a bed. Slowly he settled down into it and rested with his hands behind his head. Chak had already made a nest from his pile of hay

115

and lay curled up in it. It did not take him long to fall asleep and soon his snoring reverberated around the cave.

Jessica's eyes burned with tiredness yet she lay awake in her cradle of hay. Slowly a salty tear trickled down her cheek as she struggled with the unhappiness inside her. She was so very scared and she wondered if they would ever be rescued.

Chapter 11
Telepathy and Triceratops

Irises was leading Jessica through the gloomy tunnels. Her ankles were no longer shackled and she had to run to keep up with him. Through the winding passageways they went, never meeting another soul. They passed into the deserted main chamber and clambered up the steep, stony steps to the passage halfway up the side of the cavern's rocky walls.

Irises raced up the steps with breathtaking speed and quickly reached the top. Jessica was only midway up the staircase and her legs began to feel as though they had heavy weights attached to them.

The old man stood on the platform at the top of the stairs looking down at her with his brilliant blue eyes. His long white robes and wispy beard fluttered in the breeze from the dark passageway. Slowly he extended his gnarled hand out to her.

No matter how hard she tried, her legs just would not move. She stared up at Irises's outstretched hand. A sad look passed over the old man's wrinkled face and he withdrew his hand.

"Jessica!" he called.

⟨⟨⟨⟨⟨⟨⟩

Jessica sat up with a start.

Looking about, it was clear that she was still in the chamber with the sleeping beasts and her two friends. TJ had nestled down in his pile of hay and was gently snoring. Chak had rolled over in his sleep and now lay across Jessica's legs, which explained why her legs had felt so heavy and numb.

Disappointment welled up inside her. The dream has seemed so real, it was almost as if Irises had spoken in her ear.

In frustration she shoved Chak off her legs. Totally oblivious to her roughness he just rolled over, sighed and began snoring loudly.

⟨⟨⟨⟨⟨⟨⟩

"Jessica!"

She jumped. It was Irises again, repeating her name. Jessica looked about her frantically, eyes alert and with hope beginning to leap in her heart. All was quiet in the cave only the sound of Chak snoring like a warthog disturbed the peace.

"Is this some kind of trick?" Jessica thought to herself, too scared of waking the sleeping beast to call out loudly. "Where are you Irises?"

"Inside your mind my young friend" he replied.

"Great" she thought grimly, "not only am I shackled in this stinking cave with these two idiots, but now I'm going crazy, too!" only to hear Irises chuckling.

"No, my dear, you are not going mad. I'm using telepathy to contact you. You are very lucky to posses such a special gift, very few have it!"

"Telepathy?" she thought in wonder.

"Did you not wonder why no one else reacted when I spoke to you in levitation class and asked you to go higher?"

"I never really thought about it" she replied, frowning. "But I guess your right, no one else did react."

"That's because I used telepathy to speak to you. No one else could hear our thoughts. Now tell me, are you all ok?"

"Oh, Irises, it's horrible, we're shackled in a dark cave with these huge beasts and I'm so scared."

"Are you hurt?"

"No, none of us are hurt. Although Chak has come close to getting a thump or two!"

"Do you know where you are?"

"No" Jessica replied, sadly.

"Then you had better tell me exactly what has happened and how you got there," he said gently.

Jessica began by telling how Chak had teleported them from the alley at the bazaar out into the wastelands of the desert and then described Scarab and Tupai and their teleportation to the spaceship. She told him about their week on board the ship and their arrival at the underground tunnels. She made sure to tell him all about the strange pale, white haired slaves and the great beasts that pulled the trucks.

When she had finished her tale she waited for Irises's response. The silence stretched on and she began to fear that she had lost contact with her tutor.

CⲰⲰⲰⲰⲰⲰⲰⲰⲰⲰⲰ

"Irises are you still there?" she asked.

"Oh I'm sorry, yes I am still here; I was lost in thought. It seems you have been taken to one of the mining colonies on the outskirts of the system and an illegal mine at that. The Interplanetary Government forbids all use of slavery, but there are privateers who are known to operate such facilities whilst the authorities are tied up defending themselves against Abrath. The two men who captured you are Algebraic Warriors who have sadly become mercenaries. They have no morals and have loyalty to none. They take any work for money without regard for the consequences. I dread to think what they have done to end up owning an Elyon spaceship."

CⲰⲰⲰⲰⲰⲰⲰⲰⲰ

"What are we going to do?" asked Jessica.

"You are going to have to be brave little warriors, Jessica. I think for the time being you are in no immediate danger but we must try to rescue you as quickly as possible. The information you have given me should help me to locate you and I need all three of you to gather as much information as possible."

"But I'm scared, Irises, and these beasts are terrifying!" she whimpered.

"There is no need for you to be scared my little friend. Those beasts are triceratops and they are very gentle harmless creatures from the planet Earth and they live in the outer regions."

"Harmless! How can something with such big teeth be harmless?"

"They are herbivores, Jessica; that is what their big teeth are for"

"We have been shackled next to herbivores. Please, Irises; hurry and rescue us!" she said, beginning to panic.

"Calm down, herbivores only eat plants, they don't eat meat. Carnivorous animals eat meat. Triceratops are a very docile species Jessica, you have nothing to fear. In fact when I was a young boy there were tales of triceratops having telepathic skills, but as I have never met one, I wouldn't know if this is true. Maybe you could try your telepathic skills on them."

"OK I'll try when they wake up, but what about the slaves, do you know who they are?"

"The small pale species you described are Eridans from the planet Eridanus. They are incredibly strong little creatures that are good-natured but not too intelligent I'm afraid. Now you need to get plenty of rest. I'll contact you again soon, but in the meantime try not to cause too much trouble for your captors. It would not be a good idea to provoke them. Make sure TJ understands that!"

"What about Chak?"

"Ah yes, Chak. He must not, under any circumstances use teleportation. You are too close to Abrath's evil legions for it to be safe to use. This is very important Jessica."

"I understand, Irises, don't worry, I'll make sure he doesn't use teleportation."

"I have to go now Jessica I can't keep this link secure for much longer. I promise I will be in touch with you soon. Your parents love you all dearly. Remember that. Goodbye my little warrior."

"Oh please don't go Irises" she begged. "Help us. Tell us what to do. Irises, are you there?"

There was no response. Jessica sobbed silently not wishing to wake the others. She curled up in her pile of hay and slowly cried herself to sleep.

Irises climbed the rickety steps to reach the top shelf of the bookcase behind his chaotic desk. The old wooden steps creaked and groaned in protest as he moved around searching amongst the dusty scrolls and parchments. Eventually, after much rummaging and muttering, he found what he had been looking for and clambered back down the battered steps with the scroll clasped firmly in his gnarled hand.

He settled himself at his desk and cleared a space amongst the clutter before unrolling the scroll and placing a weight on each corner. Slowly he stroked his snowy white beard as he pored over the star chart before him. So lost in his studies was he, that he failed to notice his servant enter the room.

"I've brought you some sweet tea, Irises, and some fruit. I'm very worried about you. You've not been eating properly and you do look a bit peaky," he said, placing a laden tray next to the chart.

"It's not me you should be worrying about Gregor. It should be those missing children," replied the old man.

"Oh I am worried about them too, Irises. It's terrible. Poor little things being snatched away like that" Gregor said, wringing his hands and looking concerned.

Irises put down his magnifying glass and poured himself a cup of fragrant, steaming tea. He lifted the delicate cup to his whiskery lips and slurped loudly. Gregor tried to ignore his master's none too delicate drinking etiquette and began looking at the chart spread out on the desk.

"What's this?" he asked, as he removed a cloth from his pocket and began dusting the chart.

A huge dust cloud rose from the chart. It tickled Irises' nose and he sneezed which made him spill his tea down the front of his robes. Gregor immediately leant forward and began dabbing at the tea stain with his cloth. Irises impatiently swatted his servant's hands away.

"For goodness sake, stop fussing Gregor!" Irises said trying not to cough and splutter.

"Sorry" muttered Gregor, returning the cloth to his pocket and turning his attention back to the chart.

"So what is it?"

"It's a star chart," replied Irises as he wiped his eyes before sorting through the bowl of fruit.

"I can see it's a star chart," said the man rolling his jade green eyes, "but a star chart of where?"

"The outer system. Now if you don't mind I need some peace and quiet to work. Thank you for the tea. Oh, and the fruit" he said, picking up a juicy fat grape and popping it into his mouth.

Gregor looked hurt at his dismissal.

"Okay. Well, call if you need anything" he said taking a last glance at the chart before leaving the room.

Irises picked up his magnifying glass and resumed his studies. The map charted the outer system beyond Pluto. In this area there were a dozen small formations in orbit around the distant sun. Each was no bigger than Earth's own moon but all were known to be rich in mineral deposits.

CANNALLICO

Centuries ago the mineral richness of these mini-planets, as they were known, made them a precious possession for any civilisation. They had been the object of ferocious battles but eventually the Interplanetary Government had been formed and over the years they had taken control of most of the formerly independent mining colonies.

Using the information that Jessica had given him, Irises was going to try and calculate on which planet the children were being held captive. He had been able to track the children when they had teleported from Earth's surface to the ship that he had identified by their system of markings as a merchant trading ship. For this reason, it had not aroused the suspicion of Earth's security forces.

Jessica had told irises that they had felt the hyper drive engines of the ship kick in not long after they had arrived on board. The children's captors had obviously been keen to make a quick escape and must have used some form of cloaking device to hide the ship's hasty departure.

The entire journey had been at hyper drive speed. That had been easy for Irises to work out. Space sickness only occurred whilst travelling at hyper drive speed and as Jessica had been ill the entire journey, the engines must have been in use the whole time.

Irises studied the series of mini planets scattered in the expanse of space between Pluto and Andromeda. He creased his brow in a frown. If the ship had travelled for seven days and nights at hyper drive speed it would barely have made it past Pluto and the constant use of the cloaking system would have drained the engines, thereby reducing the distance they would have been able to cover.

∾⟩⟩⟩⟩⟩⟩⟩⟩∾

The first moon beyond Pluto is that of Charon but it seemed unlikely the ship would have managed to make it that far. Even if, by some miracle, they had reached Charon, it was one of the mining colonies monitored by the Interplanetary Government and it was unlikely the children were being held there. Irises sighed loudly in frustration and resumed stroking his long beard.

Rhill is the next mini planet beyond Charon but extensive mining exhausted the entire planet's mineral deposits centuries ago leaving it just a desolate and barren rock. The mining activities described by Jessica made this an unlikely place for them to be held captive.

Increasingly frustrated, Irises leant back in his seat and ran his hands through his long white hair. There was absolutely no way they could have made it beyond Rhill. He began to doubt his own skills at space navigation. It had been many years since he had last used his knowledge and he had to admit that in his old age he occasionally felt a little uncertain of his capabilities.

∾⟩⟩⟩⟩⟩⟩⟩⟩∾

"Come on you old fool!" he scolded himself. "This is basic navigation you should be able to do it with your eyes shut."

He rummaged around the untidy mess on his desk and amongst the overflowing drawers until he found a battered looking laser pen, a scrap of digital parchment and an ancient looking navigation calculator.

"Time for some good old fashioned calculations" he said, waggling his eyebrows and turning on the pen. The calculator spluttered and sparked but after a few faulty starts, the display screen shone brightly. Grasping the chipped pen in his gnarled fingers, Irises slowly began listing his calculations in spidery writing on the scrap of digital parchment and carefully punched the numbers into the ancient calculator.

Hyper drive engine speed = 21,250,000 miles per hour

Distance travelled in 24 hours = 21,250 000 x 24 = 510,000,000 miles

Distance travelled in one week = 251,000 000 x 7 = 3,570,000,000 miles

Distance from Earth to Pluto= 3,554,000,000 miles

So, from his calculations Irises could see that the ship would have passed by Pluto but he needed to see if they could have made it as far as Charon.

Distance travelled in 1 week = 3,570,000,000 miles minus

Distance from Earth to Pluto= 16,000,000 miles

Distance from Pluto Charon =   30,000,000 miles

Irises looked at his calculations. In one week the ship would have managed to travel past Pluto but it would only have reached halfway between Pluto and Charon. He scratched his head in confusion. It did not seem to make sense. The children were clearly being held captive in a mining colony and the only mining colonies were on the dozen mini planets between Pluto and Andromeda and yet it would have been impossible for them to make it to the first colony in just one week.

He took a sip of his tea that had gone cold and winced in disgust. Placing the cup back on the tray, he reached instead for a juicy orange from the fruit bowl and, lost in thought, slowly began to peel it. As he tried to reach a solution, the details Jessica had given him whirled around in his head.

Munching on a succulent segment of orange, he picked up the scrap of parchment and studied his written calculations. Suddenly his eyes opened wide and, spitting orange debris everywhere; he gave a cry of triumph!

Irises could not believe he had overlooked the significance of a piece of information that Jessica had given him. His calculations were correct for the distance covered by a hyper drive engine in seven days but he had forgotten about the symbols on the ship Jessica had described to him. It had been an Elyon ship.

Elyons were a highly intelligent race whose science was more advanced than other civilisations. They had developed hyper drive engines that were fifty percent faster than other hyper drive engines.

He had overlooked this in his calculations and had used the speed of an ordinary engine. With a gleam in his eye Irises turned over the scrap of parchment and began recalculating.

Elyon engine speed =   31,875 000 miles per hour

Distance travelled in 24 hours   =   31,875 000 x 24 = 765,000 000 miles

Distance travelled in 1 week =   765,000 000 x 7 = 5,355,000 000 miles

So the ship had easily travelled past Pluto and into the vast expanse of space before Andromeda. Carefully he measured out the distance on the chart. Allowing for a margin of error in the time travelled (it was unlikely they had travelled for exactly seven days), he narrowed their location down to two possible positions.

There were either on the mini planet Seno or its neighbour Ixis. Neither was currently governed by The Interplanetary Government as each was owned by privateers. A greedy, unpopular character named Pathos, who was known for his untrustworthiness in business and his many enemies over the years, owned Seno. Another privateer, an evil and cruel man by the name of Akka owned Ixis. According to rumours, Akka had murdered his own father and brother over a business disagreement

This greatly disturbed irises. The children would suffer if they were in the hands of either of these parasites. He was sure he had a book about these mini planets somewhere in his collection. Irises got up from his chair, stretched his cramped limbs and began perusing the books on the sagging shelves, occasionally taking a volume from the shelf and flicking through a few pages before replacing it.

"Making any progress?" asked Gregor, surprising the old man.

"Yes thank you" he replied.

"Good" smiled the servant, tidying the tea things and fruit peel and placing them on the tray. "I see you've been busy exercising your brain" he commented while studying the calculations on the scrap of digital paper.

"I'm afraid it has been a very long time since my poor brain did any serious calculations. It made a refreshing change to dust off all those old cobwebs," said Irises, smiling.

"I'm afraid maths was never my strong point" said Gregor, lifting up the tray, now loaded with the tea things. "Well I'd best get back to the

kitchen otherwise dinner will be burnt to a crisp"
he said taking a last, lingering look at the chart.

Irises watched his servant leave the room,
balancing the tray on one arm and pushing the
heavy door open with the other. The old man
smiled fondly. Gregor had been with him since,
as a young man, he had failed to qualify for the
Imperial University on Anapacious. They had been
through many rough times together. Irises had
Gregor to thank for some of his beloved volumes
that now filled the shelving on the walls after saving
them from the destruction Abrath had wreaked on
their planet. Irises turned his attention back to
the shelves and smiled as he spotted the book for
which he had been searching.

"I may have narrowed down the location of
these children," he thought to himself, "but there
is still so much to do. Lives will have to be put at
risk in rescuing them."

Jessica slowly sat up and rubbed her sleepy
eyes. The beasts were stirring in their stalls making
their chains clink as they moved. TJ and Chak
were awakening, too. They both had straw poking
from their hair and a slimy trail was running down
Chak's cheek where he had dribbled in his sleep.
Jessica gave him a disgusted look and wrinkled
her nose.

She stood up and began brushing off the
straw that was clinging to her grubby clothes

and carefully began pulling stalks from her hair, brushing it through with her fingers.

TJ and Chak decided to skip grooming altogether and instead, rushed to investigate the sack that had been left next to a fresh bucket of water. TJ managed to reach the cloth bag first and, before Chak's his podgy fingers could fasten on the bag, swiftly elbowed him out of the way.

Jessica sighed and decided to get a cupful of fresh water before Chak could pollute it. She took great gulps to quench her thirst and helped herself to a second cup of the cool sweet liquid.

꙰꙰꙰꙰꙰

TJ removed several hunks of grey bread from the bag and shared them with his two friends. He reached back into the bag and pulled out a parcel wrapped in shiny greasy paper. Putting his bread to one side to ensure it was out of Chak's reach, TJ carefully unwrapped the parcel.

Inside laid thick slices of some kind of fatty meat and some kind of pickled vegetable. Deciding it smelt fine, he offered some to Jessica. Now over her space sickness, Jessica was ravenous. She took a slice of meat and a pickle and—remembering her manners—thanked TJ. She put the meat on the bread and took a big bite. The meat tasted salty and she had to chew it vigorously as it was a little tough but she did not care and her stomach gurgled in delight.

Pleased to see his friend tucking in with relish, TJ then offered some meat to Chak whose beady little eyes shone with anticipation. Licking his lips, Chak picked up two slices of meat and stuffed them straight into his mouth. TJ took the remaining slice and tried to ignore the slobbering noises coming from his greedy friend.

CANNNNNO

The children sat eating in silence, watching as the cavern came to life. Some more men in red uniforms arrived in the cave and began checking over the beasts. They refreshed the grain and water troughs in each stall. None of them looked at the children and Jessica felt as though she was invisible. She finished her bread and meat as she watched the men unchain the beasts from the wall and then lead them, one by one, out of the cave.

"Could Irises be right about the possibility of finding one of these beasts with telepathic skills?" she thought to herself as she watched the rear end of the last triceratops disappear from sight around the cave entrance.

She waited a while to ensure that the men were not returning before sharing her news of Irises's contact. When she was sure it was safe she told TJ and Chak of her telepathic conversation with their tutor.

CANNNNNO

"Well?" she said, as the two boys sat in stunned silence.

"Err, look Jessica you don't think there's a small chance you dreamt it?" asked TJ tentatively.

Jessica was always convinced she was right and whenever doubt was expressed she had been known to lose her temper with unfortunate consequences for the doubter, hence TJ's reluctance to question her experience. True to form, Jessica felt heat rush to her face and she clenched her fists tightly at her sides.

"I did not dream it, thank you TJ!" she replied indignantly.

TJ and Chak looked at each other and rolled their eyes. Once again it seemed Jessica was determined to prove she was right.

"So how long did Irises say it would be until they can rescue us?" asked TJ, idly playing with a length of straw.

"He doesn't know" she replied biting her lip, "but he told me that it's important that we gather as much information as possible to help him."

"Oh, right." said TJ feeling brave and humouring her.

Chak, unfortunately, had yet to learn the fine art of tiptoeing around Jessica's temper and foolishly began sniggering and smirking. Big mistake!

"I'm telling you it's true!" she snapped, making the two boys jump. "But if you don't want to believe me, that's up to you."

"Well, it's not so much that we don't believe you; it's just that I'm not sure how we can gather information while tethered by these things" TJ explained, rattling his shackles.

"You're just jealous Irises spoke to me and not you," Jessica snapped, folding her arms tightly across her chest.

"No!" replied TJ defensively. A part of him had desperately wanted to believe Irises had been in touch but it was true; he was jealous.

"Oh yes you are" accused Jessica. "You've got the huffs because he spoke to me and not you. Let's face it; it would be a waste of time trying to contact either of you two— Boy Wonder and his sidekick Boy Blubber!"

Jessica knew immediately that she had gone too far and instantly regretted being so mean to Chak who looked at her with hurt eyes, his bottom lip beginning to tremble.

"That was nasty and spiteful, Jessica" TJ said, glaring at her. "There's no need to be quite so horrible just because we find it hard to believe your story."

The children fell into an uncomfortable silence. Jessica lay back down in her straw and turned her back on the boys. A short while later Scarab and Tupai came into the chamber.

"How are we enjoying ourselves kiddies?" asked Scarab, crouching down in front of the children.

Tupai hovered in the background looking nervous and on edge. His beady eyes darted from child to child and he tapped his grubby fingers against his leg.

"Oh we're having a ball," replied TJ sarcastically.

"Glad to hear it" said Scarab grinning. "Now if the young lady and you two gentlemen can possible tear yourselves away from these palatial surroundings there's someone wanting to see you."

"Who?" Jessica asked indignantly.

"Oh, I wouldn't want to spoil the surprise now would I?" chuckled Scarab. "I'm going to trust you not to give me any trouble. You have a choice. You can either come with me quietly and I won't have to use the kinetic bands or you can give me aggravation and I'll make sure those bands are so tight your arms will turn blue; understood?"

The children all looked at each other then slowly nodded their agreement. "I don't trust 'em" Tupai sneered, screwing up his pointy features. "You should leave their shackles on at least."

"I don't think we need to do that," said Scarab as he began undoing Jessica's shackles.

Tupai glared at the children with obvious displeasure. "No funny business" he said. "Any nonsense and the bands and shackles go back on."

Once Scarab had removed their shackles, the children massaged their ankles where the metal had rubbed their skin. With Tupai following closely behind, the children followed Scarab through the endless snaking of torch-lit corridors that would take them out of the cave. It did not take long, though, for Chak to start complaining of exhaustion.

"My legs hurt" he whined.

"Something else will hurt in a minute if you don't get a move on" snarled Tupai, prodding him in the back with his finger.

"Ow! Careful! I bruise easily you know."

"Get a move on you lazy brat."

"How can I get a move on when my poor body is close to exhaustion. I'm suffering the effects of starvation you know," said Chak, sucking in his tummy.

"Ha ha" laughed Tupai nastily. "There's no worry about you starving to death. Look at yourself. It would take a light-year for that weight to fall off you."

"Cheek!" said Chak sulkily.

"Now move!" snapped Tupai, shoving Chak forward roughly.

The corridors twisted and turned, each one looking the same as the last. The children were soon totally lost and any idea of running from their captors was ditched. Even if they could escape from the two men, they would not know in which direction to run.

Slowly the corridor widened and the sound of laughter reached the children. They passed by two men in red uniforms each holding one of the prods that the children had seen used on the pale beings. The men glared at the little group as it passed them by.

They eventually came out into another cavern. In the centre of the cavern stood a large, heavy wooden chair on which sat a giant of a man. He had a riot of curly red hair and a huge bushy red beard above which peeked his rosy cheeks. His massive hands rested on an enormous belly that hung over a thick leather belt decorated with metal symbols.

A tall, wiry looking man stood next to the Giant's chair. He was clad in sky blue robes and wore silver space boots on his long feet. His jet-black hair flowed down to rest upon his shoulders and his eyes were obscured by darkened shades that sat upon a pointy nose.

The children slowly shuffled together for comfort as Scarab walked forward and addressed the giant man.

"Here are your goods, sir. All present and correct and, as you can see, a bonus one too."

"Are they definitely the right ones?" he asked Scarab eyeing the group of bedraggled children.

"No doubt, these are the ones you wanted. The source you recommended to us was of great help and only too willing to help us to find them."

The children looked at each other in confusion.

"What's he talking about?" whispered TJ.

"I don't know" Jessica whispered back shrugging her shoulders.

Chak did not answer but just looked at his shoes and whimpered.

"Quiet" hissed Tupai behind them.

The big man murmured something to the man in the blue robes and they both laughed loudly. The giant lifted his hefty frame from the chair and strode towards the children. Chak tried to move back away from the man but found Scarab blocking his path. Jessica stood her ground whilst TJ slowly crept behind her.

"Well, well, well" boomed the big man as he stopped in front of the girl.

"What have we got here?"

"I don't know who you are or what you want but I demand that you take us back home right this instant!" said Jessica, indignantly sticking her chin forward and squaring her shoulders.

The huge man clutched his belly and let out a rumbling laugh. "My, this one has spirit" he said, with a glint in his eye. "What do you think, Rook?"

"Indeed, she seems to be a fiery one," said the wiry man.

The large man turned away from his friend to face Jessica. He bent forward and reached out his large hand to touch her head. She flinched away from him just as TJ leapt forward and began flailing his fists at the giant.

"Leave her alone!" yelled TJ pounding the man as hard as he could. The giant reached down with his huge paw and gently moved TJ away from him.

"That's enough, little man. I wasn't going to hurt your friend," he growled. "I can't sell damaged goods now can I?"

Tupai moved forward and hauled TJ away from the man. Before the boy could react his arms were pinned at his sides by kinetic bands. Wincing, he looked at Jessica and Chak and saw that they too had now been bound.

"You were warned," said Tupai, a vile grin spreading on his face. "Show some respect to your new owner."

"Owner!" spat Jessica. "We're not pets."

"No," boomed the big man, "far from being pets you are a valuable commodity and there's someone out there willing to pay generously to have possession of you."

"What are you talking about and who are you?" asked TJ, struggling against the bands pinning his arms.

"Enough questions" said the giant with a dismissive wave of his hand. "I've seen them now you can take them away!"

"Come on" said Scarab, pushing the children back out of the cavern. Remembering what Irises had told her, Jessica, strained her ears to hear what the big man was saying to Rook. She could barely make it out above the sound of their footsteps in the corridor.

"What did he say when he found out we had them?" the red haired man was asking eagerly.

"He was very pleased indeed. The deal has been agreed and believe me you will be generously rewarded," replied Rook.

"Excellent, excellent; when are you to take them?"

"A ship will be arriving in the next day or so to take them and me to him. It will also be carrying your payment on board."

"Marvellous! What about his promise of making me general of one of his mighty legions?"

Jessica strained to hear more of the conversation but their voices were now too faint. She trudged along behind the boys while running what she had heard through her mind. Who had they been talking about and why on earth would someone want to pay generously for a bunch of children? She could see Chak slumped forward and dragging his feet. Despite Tupai's mean comments earlier about his size, Chak had lost some weight and the waist of his trousers now hung low on his hips. Chak's shuffling motion and the rubbing of the kinetic band were pushing the waistband of his trousers lower so that the crack of his bottom peeked over the top and she was sure she could see the edge of a sweet wrapper poking out!

"Who would pay for that?" thought Jessica, looking away in disgust. "What would Irises make of what she had heard?"

A cold chill ran through her body. She just knew they were heading into danger. Irises had to get in touch soon

CX11111111CO

TJ shifted himself into a more comfortable position from where he could watch Jessica. He tried to believe her story of Irises contacting her but it all seemed just too farfetched. Maybe the trauma of being snatched had disturbed her mind.

He shook his head sadly as he watched her stare intently at the beast in the stall next to them. She had convinced herself that she would be able to communicate telepathically with one of the triceratops as she insisted on calling them and had spent at least two hours so far sending messages to the poor animal.

"At least it keeps her out of our hair" thought TJ, "she can be such a nag sometimes."

Chak whimpered and looked at TJ with his big brown eyes.

"No Chak" said TJ, pushing the grocery bag further away from his tubby friend. "It's your own fault for raiding the grocery bag. You will just have to wait until the men bring us some more food."

"But I'm hungry" he whined, clutching his still ample belly. "My sugar levels might fall too low and I'll slip into a coma and die or maybe I'll be too weak to walk anywhere and I'll be left here to die of starvation. Then you'll be sorry, you just see."

"Oh don't be so ridiculous. I don't know how you can possibly be hungry," snapped TJ. "After all, you have managed to empty a bag of fruit and a bag biscuits."

His friend's face reddened to a spectacular shade of scarlet as he hung his head, resting one of his many chins on his chest.

"No need to go on about it, you know," he muttered under his breath.

Tj was fuming. He had been woken during the night by the sound of Chak squirreling around in the straw and the sound of rustling wrappers. His eyes had opened just in time to see his friend stuffing a handful of biscuits into his mouth whilst rummaging in the grocery bag with the other. Momentarily forgetting his shackles, TJ had leapt up and tripped over them. Getting back to his feet, he had snatched the bag from Chak's hands. Looking inside he could see there were only vegetables left. TJ had angrily thrown the bag onto his own straw bed and glared at his friend.

Chak had guilt written all over his face and the evidence of empty biscuit and sweet wrappers littered his untidy bed of straw. His fleshy lips trembled and his eyes had filled with tears.

"Sorry" Chak mumbled, wiping his running nose.

"That food was for our escape" snapped TJ. "I can't believe you can be so greedy and as for stashing your sweets all for yourself, that's unforgivable." Through watery eyes and dribbling nose, Chak just snivelled and looked at his friend.

"You know Jessica is going to explode when she finds out about this," hissed TJ, pointing at the curled up sleeping figure of Jessica, "and when she does you're on your own."

He had been right. Jessica lost her temper in true style. Chak had not been able to get a word in edgeways as she let loose with a torrent of angry words and both the boys blushed from the tips of their toes to the roots of their hair when she used a forbidden swear word.

"Now is not the time to threaten to tell Rathooq," thought TJ wisely.

The fact that Chak had selfishly hidden and consumed his bag of sweets seemed to infuriate her even more which was worrying as she did not even like sweets!

With her fury spent and despite his feeble attempts to apologise, Jessica had totally ignored Chak for the entire day. The children had not been visited again and the men ignored them when they returned with the beasts after a long shift in the mines.

Jessica had turned her attention to the triceratops in the stall next to theirs and was standing silently looking at the beast. It, on the other hand did not appear to be paying any attention to the girl. It was too busy sniffing around the nearby food trough, clearly hungry from a hard day's work.

TJ suddenly felt sorry for her and a wave of pity washed over him. He could tell she was miserable. She looked so shabby and unlike the immaculate Jessica he had come to love and hate. Her hair and clothes were a mess and, if he were to be honest, they could all do with a good bath, even though he was not too fond of them. She was always so fussy about her appearance and he smiled remembering the times she insisted he wait for her whilst she stopped at a clothes stall at the bazaar on the way home from the academy.

He reached into the grocery bag and pulled out a spiky looking vegetable called a jojo. Getting to his feet he shuffled across the stall towards Jessica as far as his shackles would allow.

"He might want to be friends if you offer him this," he suggested, holding out the purple vegetable. Jessica looked down at the jojo then back up at TJ.

"It's worth a try I suppose," she said shrugging her shoulders and taking it from his hand.

Straining against the shackles, she leant forward and tossed the jojo over the partition into the triceratops stall. The beast lifted his head from the trough and sniffed at the jojo lying amongst the straw on the floor. Gently it picked it up in its big teeth and began chewing on it whilst watching the children with one of its yellow eyes.

"He seems to like it," said Jessica watching intently.

"Here give him another" said TJ, passing her a second jojo. "See if he'll take it from your hand."

"You see if it'll take it from your hand, there's no way I'm going anywhere near those teeth" she said, passing it back and tugging at his shackles.

"Come on just try."

"Oh, okay" she said turning back towards the beast.

She came face to face with its nose and leapt back towards TJ.

"See, look he wants some more" said TJ, pushing her forward.

"It might be a she," she said pushing back against her friend's hands.

The triceratops' nostrils quivered as it sniffed the air for scent of the jojo.

"Go on" TJ said, shoving her towards the beast.

Jessica stumbled forward and gingerly stretched out her open hand with the spiky jojo sitting on her palm. The triceratops grunted and looked at her warily. Ever so slowly it opened its mouth and moved towards Jessica.

Shaking with fear Jessica closed her eyes tightly as she felt the animal's warm breath on her arm. She felt something soft gently brush against her hand and she peeked from one open eye. The triceratops was happily munching on the vegetable, Jessica was sure she could see it smiling.

TJ looked pleased that his idea had worked. Maybe the animal's newfound interest in Jessica would cheer her up a bit.

"I wonder what his name is?" whispered TJ.

"Who knows?" she replied. "Do you think he would mind much if I stroked him?"

"Mmmm, I'm not sure you should do that," replied TJ, eyeing the triceratops' large teeth. "Just try giving him another jojo".

TJ turned around to reach for the grocery bag but it wasn't there. Chak was clutching it to his heaving chest.

"Don't give it any more. You were angry with me for touching the food in here and yet you're happily feeding it to ... to ... that thing" he said, waving his hand in the direction of the triceratops.

"Don't be so stupid, Chak," said TJ frowning, "there are only vegetables left and none of them can be eaten raw; well not by us anyway."

"But I can't survive purely on the food they are giving us here" whined Chak, "I'm a growing lad with a healthy appetite!"

"Growing outwards" muttered Jessica under her breath. TJ struggled not to laugh.

"It won't do us any harm to befriend these animals, we might need them to help us escape" explained TJ.

"Escape?" snorted Chak. "What chance of escape do we have? Firstly, in case you hadn't noticed our ankles are chained to the wall. Secondly, we would never find our way to the surface through that maze of tunnels and thirdly, I think that giant who seems keen to sell us will ensure the guys with the prods don't let us get away. Anyway, even if we did overcome all of that, I don't know how you imagine we would get away from this planet seeing as none of us can fly a space ship! "

"Well thank you so much for those positive points" replied TJ, standing with his hands on his hips. "At least we were trying to do something other than feel sorry for ourselves. Jessica told us what those men were saying. We are to leave with that man Rook any day now so we have to try and come up with some sort of plan.

"Maybe it would be more helpful if you tried to think of a plan instead of picking holes in everything. After all, we are in this together," said Jessica, absently patting the triceratops that was now nuzzling her hand. TJ and Chak stared at her in amazement.

"Now what's wrong?" she asked.

"Look what you are doing," stuttered TJ, pointing behind her.

Jessica slowly looked around and realised she had been patting the great beast.

"Oh!" was all she could say.

"I think he wants to be friends," said TJ, smiling.

He reached over and picked up the grocery bag that Chak had dropped in surprise.

"Here, give him one final jojo," he said handing her one last spiky vegetable before storing the bag in his own bed.

The animal took the jojo and again began nuzzling Jessica's hand as it munched on the purple jojo. Jessica laughed and began stroking the beast's neck. TJ was pleased to see his friend smiling as he sat back on this bed and watched her stroking and tickling the animal.

Chak sat staring open-mouthed.

"Pssst" hissed TJ, "stop staring and get thinking."

"Okay" muttered Chak, still gawking.

Later as the triceratops settled down to sleep, a man in red overalls brought the children a sack of food and some fresh water. The man refused to speak to the children and left after his delivery, ignoring the questions they put to him.

TJ took the sack and divided its contents equally between the three of them. The children tucked into the bread and greasy meat and washed it down with cold, sweet water.

"I've been thinking about an escape plane," said Jessica popping the last of her bread into her mouth.

"Oh no, here we go again" muttered Chak, wiping the back of his hand across his mouth and smearing grease up his cheek.

"Be quiet Chak. You haven't come up with any suggestions," said TJ.

"Well, I was thinking if we could escape just after the beasts have been taken to the mines, we could follow them and get to the main chamber."

"How would we follow them? They move much faster than we do" interrupted Chak.

"Unless your nose has failed you recently they smell awful and I'm sure we're all capable of following piles of steaming dung!" Jessica replied, making Chak gag at the prospect. "Anyway, as I was saying, if we could get to the main chamber then hide somewhere until the shift changes. Then, we could climb those steps unnoticed. All we'd have to do is follow the corridor to the surface."

"I'm sure the men with those prods will notice us climbing up the steps." said Chak, picking his teeth.

Jessica wrinkled her nose in disgust.

"Do you have to do that?"

"Yes I've got meat stuck in my teeth. I've got toothache as it is I don't want to make it any worse" he replied, digging again with his podgy finger.

"I'm not surprised you've got toothache eating sweets when there's no way to brush your teeth. I'll bet they're rotten," she said pulling a sour face.

"Oh shut up Miss Perfect; just because I've found a mistake with your plan."

"Okay that's enough, both of you," said TJ making calming gestures with his hands. "Go on Jessica, what about the men spotting us?"

"Well they won't if there's a diversion" she replied, smiling.

"Okay" said TJ slowly "how will we create a diversion?"

"Oh that's easy. We don't do anything," she answered.

TJ and Chak looked at each other blankly.

"So let me get this right," said Chak, looking bemused. "We follow the triceratops to the main cavern, hide from the men, and then don't create a diversion to cover our escape?"

"That's right," she said grinning.

"Maybe I'm missing something here," said TJ looking puzzled. "Surely we need to create a diversion or the men will spot us."

"No. We don't create it, silly. The triceratops will," replied Jessica, as though it was obvious.

"Right" said TJ looking at her as though she was mad. "So we will just get the triceratops to make a diversion for us."

"We don't have to get them to do it, they just will."

"I admire your confidence but how do you know they'll just do it?"

"Because" said Jessica, rolling her eyes and sighing with frustration; "because they told me so!"

The boys gazed at her open mouthed, stunned. Chak recovered his senses first. He slapped his forehead with the palm of his hand and groaned.

TJ was lost for words.

"They told you so," repeated Chak eventually.

"Yes" she replied smiling. "Irises's was only partially right. They are all telepathic not just a few. Mind you they can be a bit unsociable until you get to know them but they're a really nice bunch once you do."

"A nice bunch?" said Chak, turning to TJ. "She's really lost it now. We're shackled with a loony!"

"I'm not a loony. I'm telling you the truth!" She said grumpily as she folded her arms across her chest.

"Oh yes you are!"

"Oh no, I'm not."

"Are!"

"Not!"

"Okay that's enough you two," said Tj, coming out of his trance and stepping between the two of them. "Let's just suppose Jessica is telling the truth."

Jessica started to protest and Chak snorted loudly.

"Let's just suppose she is," continued TJ talking over them. "There's one problem I think we've overlooked."

"What?" asked the pair in unison?

"How do we get free of these?" he asked, lifting his leg and jangling his shackles.

"Ah, yes" said Jessica "that was the part I was kind of stuck on."

"Okay, well I don't want to state the obvious but if we don't get free of these shackles the rest of your plan is useless," said TJ in exasperation.

"Don't worry, I'm sure the triceratops will tell her what to do" laughed Chak.

Jessica launched herself at Chak but luckily for him, her chained ankles stopped her just short of reaching him.

"Now, now; no need to be so touchy" he mocked.

"That's enough!" yelled TJ—disturbing the slumbering beasts. "I suggest we all just calm down and sleep on it."

The three of them returned to their straw beds and made themselves comfortable. Jessica kept glaring at Chak and he kept poking his tongue out at her to tease her. Eventually, one by one, they fell into a troubled slumber.

Chapter 12
Hopes Dashed

Irises pushed back the covers of his sleeping pod, raised his body and sat with his wrinkled feet hanging over the side. His hair stood on end and his long snowy beard was a mass of tangles and knots. Lowering himself to the floor and sliding his feet into his soft slippers, he was glad to immediately feel their warmth that helped ease the stiffness of his aged joints. He reached into the cupboard next to his sleeping pod and removed a huge maroon cloak, wrapping it around his hunched shoulders to cover his faded and threadbare sleeping robes.

Slowly he shuffled from his sleeping chamber, through the hushed corridors and into his crowded study. His eyes were bloodshot over their huge bags and his pale skin shone as he switched on a single lamp over his desk.

The old man picked up a grey dust covered book from the pile on his desk and began leafing through the pages. Carefully he read through the information, muttering to himself before licking his finger and turning the page. He was so very tired yet unable to sleep for more than a few minutes at a time. He needed to verify his estimations before he could contact the children.

Hours before he had used telepathy to contact a few trusted people to help find and rescue the children. His hopes of assistance from Andromeda were dashed as he learnt that it had finally fallen to Abrath's evil forces. The surviving Andromedians had fled to Pluto and beyond, as had the Anapacion refugees years before.

The children were now in extreme danger and their rescue was of the utmost urgency. He had only one option left and it was a huge risk to take. If it failed, many years of hard work and suffering could be snuffed out in an instant and the children would be left to the mercy of Abrath.

Irises looked in the direction of the trunk stowed in the corner of his study. He could barely make out the shape of the carved box with its cyberlock glowing dimly in the darkness. Once more he cursed it and the burden of responsibility that it brought to bear upon his shoulders.

Turning his attention back to the volume in front of him, he flicked over the page and immediately what he had been looking for leapt out from the facts and figures on the page. He carefully read the details several times, constantly checking them against his notes. Now that he had the facts he needed, it was time for action. He sat back in his chair and began to control his breathing. His mind started searching for the telepathic link; to the only one who could now help. The communication would have to be kept brief to reduce the risk of detection. Then Irises would contact the children.

He could only hope he was not too late.

⌒\\\\\\\⌒

Scarab and Tupai led the children along one of the many dingy corridors. Neither had offered any explanation to the youngsters when they had removed their shackles and led them from the stall. All three children did as they were told and caused no trouble. None of them wanted to again feel the crushing pressure of the kinetic bands that Tupai delighted in using as a threatened punishment for any perceived misdemeanour.

In the distance they could hear a loud rumbling and the air was beginning to smell damp and musty. The noise grew louder and louder until they turned a corner and it became a deafening roar. The children pressed their hands to their ears and gasped in amazement at the sight before them.

They had entered a huge underground chamber through which ran a fast moving river. The water bubbled and boiled angrily as it raced through to its destination. A huge pile of buckets—the same as the one that contained their drinking water—sat on the rocky bank where they now stood. The buckets were being filled one by one by a few of the pale Eridans who dangled them into the fast moving water, swinging them back on to the bank once they were full. Two men in red overalls watched over the Eridans, each clutching one of the dreaded prods.

As he could not shout loud enough to be heard over the roar of the river, Tupai indicated with hand signals that the children were to each take one of the full buckets and follow Scarab. The buckets were heavy and the children struggled to carry them as they made their way down the riverbank that was slippery from the green slime with which it was covered. Scarab led them down towards a large wooden screen and Tupai followed them close behind.

Tupai hustled Chak to move faster as his feet slipped and slid on the slime and water sloshed from his bucket. Suddenly Chak's feet flew out from beneath him and he began to flail around trying to regain his balance. Water sprayed out from Chak's bucket in an arc that drenched TJ and Jessica and the bucket hit Tupai on the nose. Chak continued to keep a grip on its handle as Tupai's fingers clutched at what he thought was left of his nose. Tears of pain ran down his cheeks and his eyes blazed angrily at Chak. The sound of the river roared around them, drowning out Tupai's curses and Chak's grovelling apologies.

Grabbing Chak by the collar with one bloody hand, Tupai led the blubbering boy back along the slimy path towards the Eridans. Chak's large frame wobbled as he blubbered at being taken back to collect another bucketful of water.

Scarab continued on followed by TJ and Jessica who were dripping wet. They were glad to get off the slippery pathway and behind the screen. The roaring of the river quietened a little and once they were led into the small cavern adjacent to the screen, the sound was no longer so loud and they could hear themselves talk.

The cavern was bare except for a wooden bench along one of the walls. The floor sloped downwards toward the middle of the room where there was a hole, about the same size as an orange.

Scarab lifted a large black bag from his shoulder and placed it on the end of the bench. He untied the straps and began removing the contents and placing them carefully in three neat piles next to the bag. Each pile consisted of neatly folded brown material and a small green waxy looking object on the top.

⌒\\\\\\\\⌒

Chak appeared at the entrance to the cavern closely followed by Tupai. With his face flushed from crying, Chak was panting with the exertion of carrying the heavy bucket. He placed the bucket on the hard rock floor and let out a huge sigh of relief.

"Okay, kiddies," said, Scarab looking at the children, "Master Rook has decided that he cannot possibly deliver such a smelly, dirty bunch of brats so its bath time for you lot! There's some clean clothes there," he said, pointing at the neat piles, "and some soap. You need to hurry as the next shift of workers is due soon to clean up after working the mines. My friend and I will wait outside whilst you wash yourselves."

"How are we supposed to dry ourselves?" asked Jessica indignantly. "We're not here to pamper you" Tupai sneered as he wiped at the drying blood on his face with a grimy cloth. "You'll just have to put your clean clothes on top of your wet skin."

"I can't do that!" argued Chak. "I have to be careful with my delicate health. If I go around sopping wet I could catch a chill, maybe even pneumonia and I dread to think what it will do to my skin."

"You'll catch a clip around the ear in a minute" hissed Tupai through clenched yellow teeth. "Now get on with it!"

The two men turned and left the cave leaving the children staring at each other with their buckets of water on the floor in front of them.

"I'm not getting undressed in front of you two"Jessica said.

"Well, I've no intention of getting undressed in front of you either!" retorted Chak, folding his arms across his chest.

"Well I don't want to undress in front of either of you but it looks like we have no choice," said TJ, looking exasperated. "Thanks to you Chak, old Tupai's in a right foul mood and I don't think he's going to put up with any messing about!"

"It wasn't my fault!" he protested. "It was slippery. I could have ended up falling in that river and being swept away."

"We should be so lucky," muttered Jessica under her breath.

"Well how come Jessica and I managed to do it without falling over?" asked TJ.

"Oh, of course; you two are just so perfect. It's always my fault. Don't you worry about my feelings or bad health."

"It is always your fault!" said TJ angrily. "This whole mess began by us trying to rescue you. You teleported us out into the desert and you have eaten all of our emergency food supplies. What more can I say?"

"Oh, it's like that is it?" said Chak, trying to square up to his friend. Tupai shouting from the mouth of the cavern interrupted their argument. "Hurry up will you. We haven't got all day!"

"Look," said Jessica trying to calm both the boys down, "we'd better get a move on. Tupai 's in bad enough mood as it is. Why don't we place our buckets in a large triangle shape? We can stand in the middle with our backs to each other then none of us has to look at the others."

"Ok" said Chak reluctantly "but what about getting our clothes off the bench to get dressed?"

"I'll place my bucket facing the bench and when I'm done I'll go over and dress. Then I'll face the wall with my eyes shut so one of you can come over and dress. Then once their eyes are shut the last one can get dressed, okay?" she asked.

"Okay" answered Chak unenthusiastically "but no peeking!"

"Believe me, there is no danger of any peeking!" she muttered.

The children moved their buckets into position and Jessica handed out the pieces of soap. With their backs to each other they undressed and began washing with the harsh smelling soap and the freezing water.

After washing her body, Jessica decided to try and wash her long dark hair. The result was a sopping wet tangle but she was just glad it was clean. She went over to one of the piles of clothes and unfolded the first item that was a simple tunic top. She pulled it on over her head and wet hair and tied it around the waist. The material was rough and scratchy and stuck uncomfortably to her wet skin. She put on the baggy trousers made of the same material and pulled the drawstrings of the waistband before knotting them tightly. The sleeves and trouser legs were too long and she had to roll them up. Finally she put her boots back on and fastened them. Turning to face the wall she closed her eyes and told Chak he could dress.

Tupai's voice rang out again at the cavern entrance. "For the last time hurry up!"

Chak squeezed into his clothes; the tunic stretched across his tummy and, despite being too long, the trousers fitted very snugly around his waist. After much grumbling and adjusting he put on his boots and joined Jessica facing the wall with his eyes shut. TJ came over to the bench and scrambled into his clothes and boots as quickly as he could as he had started to shiver waiting for the others to dress.

"Are you ready?" yelled Tupai

Jessica was just about to shout back when TJ clamped his hand over her mouth. She gave him a puzzled look.

"I've had an idea. Leave it to me" he whispered.

"Almost" he yelled back, "just give us a couple of minutes, Chak's not quite dressed."

TJ turned back to Jessica and Chak with a wild gleam in his eye.

"Quickly" he whispered, "untie your boots and tuck in excess material of the legs of your trousers inside them. Really pad it out as much as you can before you refasten the boots."

They did as he said and as quickly as possible. TJ reached over and picked up Chak's bar of soap from next to the bucket.

"Chak, why is your bar of soap bone dry?" he asked, looking puzzled.

"I ... err ... um... well" spluttered Chak.

TJ jumped at a sound coming from the entrance. He looked at the piece of dry soap and popped it into his mouth just before Scarab and Tupai came back into the cavern.

"Don't scrub up bad, do they?" said Scarab grinning.

"I suppose not" replied Tupai. "Right you lot; put your dirty clothes in a bundle and pick up those buckets."

The children did as they were told. Scarab placed the bundle of grubby clothes in his bag and reached for the pieces of green soap.

"Hang on a minute" he said, there should be three here. Where's the other one gone?"

TJ's face was slowly turning green and being possibly the worst liar in the world, he immediately looked guilty. Jessica looked at him then stepped forward a pace.

"Oh I'm sorry, that was my fault. I dropped it on the floor when I rinsed my hair and before I could stop it the soap slid down the slope and disappeared down that hole in the floor. Sorry!" she said smiling sweetly.

"How clumsy of you!" sneered Tupai.

The two men went over and peered down the hole, looking for the soap. TJ took advantage of their backs being turned and spat the soap out into his hand. He quickly hid it in the folds of material where he had rolled up his sleeves. The two men turned their attention back to the children.

"You might as well tip your dirty water down that drain hole too, and hurry up. You've wasted too much time at it is."

The children did as they were told and followed the men back out to the slippery bank. As soon as they left the cave the roar of the river filled their ears. Several Eridans were waiting beside the screen with buckets of clean water to be taken into the cave. The children passed them by and made their way back, walking alongside the turbulent river. They handed over their empty buckets and headed back up the dingy corridor, passing several dirt-covered men in overalls heading towards the river.

⊂\\\\\\⊃

It was a miserable walk back to the children's sleeping quarters. The brown material of their clothes itched and scratched their skin. The waistband of Chak's trousers was tight and cut into his stomach. The material tucked into their boots pinched and hurt where the creases pressed into their skin.

Once back in their stall, Scarab and Tupai refastened their shackles squeezing the excess material tucked into their boots even more tightly. Scarab removed the bundle of their dirty clothes and placed it next to Jessica's school bag in the corner of the stall.

"This, my little friends, is where we say goodbye" said Scarab. "My friend and I will be collecting our payment from Pathos for delivering you and then we will be heading off tomorrow in our spaceship."

"Why do you do it?" asked Jessica.

"Why do I do what?" asked Scarab, looking puzzled.

"Why are you a mercenary? Is money all you care about?"

Tupai shifted uncomfortably and folded his arms defensively across his chest. Scarab looked thoughtful and took his time before replying in a serious tone.

"People's beliefs and motivations can be very complicated, little girl. Money isn't the most important thing to me, but it helps. Maybe I just prefer to look after myself rather than get caught up in someone else's cause!"

The children and Tupai were silent, reflecting on Scarab's explanation.

"Anyway," he said, breaking the moment, "I don't know why I'm telling you that. I don't need to explain myself to you or anyone, come to that. Good luck kiddies. You're going to need it!"

With that the two men walked away, past the empty animal stalls before leaving the cavern without as much as a backward glance. The three children looked at each other.

"Why are we going to need luck?" asked Chak, frowning.

"It's probably best we don't know," replied Jessica gloomily. "TJ, why did you make us put our trousers legs inside our boots? My ankles are really hurting."

"Mine too;" whined Chak, "and now the shackles are back on again, its even worse. Great one, TJ!"

"Did either of you figure a way to get the shackles off?" asked TJ.

Jessica and Chak shook their heads.

"Thought so," said Tj, smirking. "Well I have. With the extra material wedged inside our boots it makes our ankles seem bigger than they are. So when the shackles are on they are actually looser then they would normally be. Once we've loosened out our boots and pulled out the material the shackles will be loose enough for us to slide off our boots and hopefully pull our feet free". Jessica looked at TJ and grinned.

"Brilliant!" she said. "Come on, let's do it."

"Okay, but once you've done it you'll have to put the shackles and your boots back on. We can't let them see we can get free," he explained.

"Why can't we make a run for it now?" asked Chak as he enthusiastically tugged at the material trapped inside his boot.

"Because we need to wait until the triceratops go on their next shift. I already told you," Jessica replied indignantly.

"Oh I forgot," mocked Chak, rolling his eyes and slapping his forehead.

"Look if you don't believe me, that's your problem" snapped Jessica, "but the way things are going, we need to escape soon and unless you can think of a better plan I suggest we follow mine."

"She's right" agreed TJ, "and I've been thinking that if we are lucky we might get to stow away on Scarab and Tupai's ship before they leave.

"Oh no, not them again" moaned Chak.

"Well what choice do we have? Can you fly a spaceship?" asked TJ.

"Look, I've got my boots off but it's really a tight squeeze to get my feet out of the shackles," said Jessica.

"Ah ha!" said TJ triumphantly producing the cake of green soap from the folds of his sleeve. Rub your ankles with this. It'll make it slippery."

TJ handed the soap to Jessica. She took the green bar and began rubbing it on one of her ankles and the shackle encircling it.

"It's no good, it needs to be wet. Here" she said handing it to Chak "wet it with some of our drinking water."

Chak grasped the soap in his podgy fingers and plunged it straight into the bucket of water. Jessica and TJ looked on in disbelief as suds began to float to the surface.

"Nice one Chak" said TJ peevishly, "now our drinking water will taste lovely!"

"Well how else am I supposed to wet it?" he asked defensively.

"You could have just poured a cupful of water over the soap" suggested Jessica.

"Oh yes, I suppose I could have done. Sorry. Here you are."

Chak held out the soap to Jessica, clasping it firmly in his podgy hand. He squeezed too hard and the soap flew out of his hand, past Jessica and TJ who both lunged for it but missed. It landed in the pile of hay in the stall opposite the one they were in, and way beyond their reach.

The three of them stared in horror.

"I...I.....I'm s..." began Chak.

"Don't even say it" said Jessica tightly.

"But ...."

"No; just shut up before I shut you up."

Chak stuck his bottom lip out and held his head in his hands while he grizzled.

Jessica tried once more to free her ankles from the shackles but was unsuccessful. She gave up, defeated, and slid her boots back on.

TJ had managed to free one foot but the other, frustratingly, would not slide free of the shackle. Chak, too, had freed only one foot and was putting his boots back on, stopping every so often to wipe his running nose. TJ sighed as he put the shackle back on his free ankle and began fastening his boot.

Too disappointed to speak, the three children sat in gloomy silence.

Acknowledgements

For the help in the creation of this book, I am grateful to: the Lord our master and heavenly father for without him nothing is possible, Maxine and Michele for our constant mood changes;

Devon, Wayne and Richard in helping us full fill the dream;

Jeanette and Anita for listen to me bore you through many lunches;

Michael Anyanwu for the battle between Irieses and Abrath;

Oliver Caspersen for the children walking through the alleyway;

And finally, Terry and Zachary for creation of the Shadowfire universe.

Printed in the United Kingdom
by Lightning Source UK Ltd.
107666UKS00001B/112-174